PANTHER VALLEY TALES

BY
JAMES HALDEMAN

ILLUSTRATED BY EDGAR MCKEEVER

Eric McKeever, Publisher • Baltimore, MD

*Remember always the day
of the rope, June 21st
1877*

James E. Haldeman

Dedication

To Mr. Bernard Coleman of Tamaqua, affectionately know to me as Da.....

Edited by Sidney H. Moore, Laurel, Maryland
CyberINK (http://www.webfrog.com/cyberink/)

Technical Direction by James Skinner, Baltimore, Maryland
(jimflexx@aol.com)

Published by Eric McKeever, Baltimore, Maryland
(http://www.minecountry.com)

First Printing 1997, Thomson-Shore, Inc., Dexter, Michigan, USA
(http://www.tshore.com)

Copyright 1997 by James C. Haldeman
(http://members.aol.com/Seamus215/Panther.html)

ISBN Number 0-9643905-1-5

Library of Congress number pending

Table Of Contents

List of Illustrations

FOREWORD

In all of the United States history there is no more of a complex and tangled series of events than that of the Molly Maguire era in the coal fields of northeastern Pennsylvania. To the person content with answers to complex issues that are quick, easy, and simple, there is no problem here at all. In this view, the Mollies were a band of Irish thugs and terrorists who inflicted arson, robbery, and mayhem on their neighbors for the sheer amusement of it, and who were brought to justice by a brave and clever Pinkerton detective. That 20 Irish miners met death on the gallows seems and unbelievable penalty for idle thuggery. Perhaps there is more to this than meets the eye at a glance.

There is indeed far more to the story. The earliest efforts to organize miners labor unions were a part of it. Thirty-five thousand anthracite coal miners perished in the first century of coal mining in this region. There is no explanation or justification for a fatality rate on this scale in an established industry. There is no other industry that compares to it for death and injury of the workers. The miners attempted even in the earliest days to form unions to promote safer working conditions and a fair wage. Their efforts were met with fanatical resistance on the part of mine owners and operators.

Child labor laws were unknown and unwanted. Little boys of 8 and 9 years of age worked full time as breaker boys (slate pickers) for a pittance of a few cents an hour. In a few years they would become laborers or miners to work out their lives in brutal toil and deadly danger. A mule was worth $500, an Irish boy or man was worth nothing.

In the decades of the 1860's and 1870's in the coal counties of Northumberland, Schuylkill and Carbon, the animosities and labor strife became deadly. There were slayings of miners and mine operators both by assailants known and unknown. It became a custom and pattern to attribute all coal region crimes to Mollies no matter where the outrage occurred or who the perpetrators might be. There was the burning of breakers and the destruction of mine property, and the wrecking of trains. There were class, ethnic and religious conflicts in progress throughout this period. The focal point of all this contention was the Molly Maguire trials. They were held amid a period of anti-Irish hysteria and there was little pretense of giving anyone a fair trial.

More than a century later, who was guilty and to what degree cannot be determined in many of the cases. Information that would have changed the outcome of some of the trials is coming to light in recent years. Indeed, some of the trials may well not have taken place at all by contemporary legal standards. The detective who was the principal figure in the hanging of most of those executed turns out to be an agent provocateur, who played an active role in planning crimes and carrying them out. The alleged leader of the Mollies, John Kehoe, received a full pardon posthumously a century later.

This collection of stories is not intended to be a scholarly or academic factual presentation, though the stories are all based upon actual historical events. In some of the stories the author assigns himself the role of a participant in the events taking place, the better to convey impressions and feelings of those involved at the time and place. Academic writing permits no such latitude, and, unhappily, the study of history all to often becomes dry and dusty on that account.

The stories here will give a vivid feel for the lives and times of the miners. To the person unfamiliar with the mining industry, they will be informative. To the person more familiar with it, they will give a more complete picture and a deeper understanding. To all, they will provide some very interesting and enjoyable reading.

Eric McKeever, Publisher
Baltimore, Maryland 1997

INTRODUCTION

James Haldeman is one of the few people who can be called an authority on the folklore of the Pennsylvania coal mining regions. He knows all about the mine bosses and the miners; about the Molly Maguires and the Coal and Iron Police; and about the leading personalities that were featured in all the books, articles and documentaries that have tried to explain the murderous confrontation between big business and labor back in the 1870s.

Haldeman first became interested in the folklore of the region when he was tracking down a number of Irish ancestors who came to the coal regions in the 1850s and 1860s and later became involved in the bloody labor struggle that erupted in these regions.

The author not only gathered information about his ancestors, he also gathered a number of fascinating tales about the events and conflicts that were part of the miner's experience in that era, and during the last couple of years he has been writing stories based on the folklore he has gathered and has been publishing them in the Valley Gazette and on the Internet- on the Molly Maguire Board on AOL (America Online).

The tales are fascinating and cover a wide range of subject matter, from graphic portraits of the execution of some of the Mollies, to portraits of some of Haldeman's Irish ancestors. He also includes reviews of some current books on the Mollies, and in some instances he recreates historical events by using his imagination to bring to life cold records of the archives.

"Panther Valley Tales" will be enjoyed by anyone with an interest in the Molly Maguires or in the folklore of the coal regions. It contains a lively collection of stories that will do much to give the reader the flavor of those bygone days.

Patrick Campbell
Jersey City, New Jersey

STORIES

The Irish of Summit Hill

Overlooking Panther Valley in Summit Hill, Pennsylvania stands the Church of St. Joseph, considered by many the mother church of Panther Valley. In the beginning, St. Joseph's was just a small wooden structure heated by an old potbellied stove. The church was built In the 1840's by a group of Irish immigrants fleeing the famine in Ireland. Thomas Connahan provided the first shelter for the flock in an old stable on Pump Street. Many of the first settlers to Summit Hill came from County Donegal — from towns such as Dungloe, Glenties, Ardara, Burtonport and Innsifree. One of the most influential immigrants was Condy Cannon; he ran the Donegal Boarding House in the village of Hacklebernie. Later on, he located his hotel in Summit Hill. He sponsored many an Irishman looking for work in the mines. Condy would make them feel welcome after their long walk from Whitehouse Station in New Jersey, setting them up with food and lodging until they found work.

Over in Summit Hill, many of the new Irish families were moving to Back Street, now called Iron Street, where they would set up vegetable patches to grow enough food to supplement their daily requirements of nourishment. Often they traded with each other for different items of food and tools. Money was very scarce and bartering was the mainstay of existence. Much of the water supply came from the springs at Rickerts Grove, from the artesian wells.

In 1826 Fathers Courtney, Cummings and Fitzpatrick came by horseback from Pottsville to say mass for the Irish settlers in Summit Hill. In 1849 Father Maloney began the organization of St. Joseph's Parish. He built the first schoolroom, in the cellar of the church. Most important, he began the marriage register in June of 1850. The first marriage was that of Patrick Sharp and Margaret Mallory. Their best man was James Joolan and the bridesmaid was Joan Simpson. The next couple to be married were Patrick Brennan and Kate Sweeney. The first baptized was Rose King in May of 1850. In 1850 there were 14 more marriages; and in the following year 20 couples joined lives at St. Joseph's.

During the Civil War Father Magorien guided the flock. The war saw many of Summit Hill's sons taken away to fight against their will. They had just arrived in America, were not yet citizens, and were drafted into the armed service. Many a poor Irishman was torn away from his home, his wife and children left without financial support. This was done in a most cruel manner: they were chained in large numbers like slaves to the saddles of Dragoons and marched off to Pottsville and forced into military service. Some of their names were: Charles Kelley, John Breslin, Patrick Boyle, Patrick Gallagher, Patrick Eliot, James Moran, Christian Haldeman, Patrick Gildea, Dennis Boyle, James Furey, James O'Neal, John O'Donnell, and Martin King, who deserted later on and was never heard from again.

Following this story is a map of St. Joseph's early burial ground. (The burial ground was covered over in 1959 by Father Loughlin.) One of the parish men (Joe Buck O'Donnell) drew up a chart indicating where the early settlers of Summit Hill were laid to rest. The map indicates the final resting place of Alexander Campbell and Thomas Fisher, two men accused and executed for being Molly Maguires. Missing from this chart are the plots of my Brennan family, our first Irish ancestors to come to America in 1848. Patrick, his wife Kate, and their young daughter Anne are all buried in this cemetery. They were most likely buried without markers, or the markers have since deteriorated.

Tombstone for Hanged Mollies

From the Mauch Chunk Democrat,

Saturday September 21, 1878

Mister J. J. Rumberger has just completed a headstone to be placed on the grave of Patrick Hester at Beaver Dale, Pa. near Mount Carmel. The headstone is of Gothic design with a heavy wreath encircling a rustic cross, beneath which is the inscription in raised letters, surrounded by a heavy raised panel. On top of the headstone is the Celtic cross. The stone rests on a heavy molded base. The stone will be taken to Beaver Dale and put up some time next week.

Mister J. J. Rumberger has also nearly finished a headstone for Alexander Campbell, who was executed at Mauch Chunk. This stone is over seven feet high, has a plain finish with a Celtic cross on the top and representation of the crucifixion. The inscription on the stone is simply the name "Campbell" in heavy raised letters on the base. The complete stone weighs about a ton. It will be taken to Summit Hill, Carbon County, where Campbell is buried, in the later part of next week. A large number of persons have called at Mr. Rumberger's yard to take a look at these headstones. (*Shamokin Times*)

A Visit to Buck Mountain

One of the more enjoyable facets in doing genealogy is going on field trips to areas you usually only read about. After sitting in front of a computer, for too long a time, its good to combine a day of researching with some time out in the fresh air traveling the back roads of Carbon County. The objective for this particular afternoon was finding the site of the old Carbon County poorhouse at Laurytown. After a quick lunch at the Pub in Jim Thorpe I set out for the bad lands of Carbon County. My trip took me up state highway 93 and into the wilds of Broad Mountain. At the turn off for Weatherly I left Route 93. Weatherly is a beautiful little town secretly tucked away in the upper slopes of the County. After stopping for directions to Laurytown, I continued out through a place called Buck Mountain. A very nice old gent there gave me a rundown of the town and if I had blinked I would have missed it. I took a short side trip and started up the road to Eckley. On the old geodetic survey map I was using, Eckley wasn't listed, but a place called "Shingletown" was. Later I found out Eckley was originally called "Shingletown," and "Fillmore" in honor of President James Millard Fillmore. Back then, it was a frontier town, where shingles were made from the bark of the numerous trees dotting the landscape. The discovery of "black diamonds" changed all that forever. I often like to spend a few hours at the old village, talking informally with the tour guides. From one of these discussions I learned of the old German cemetery beyond the crumbling breaker built by Paramount Pictures in 1968 for the filming of the movie "The Molly Maguires."

From the naturalization files at the courthouse I found an ancestor from Ireland by the name of Bryan James King, whose destination was Eckley. I thought I would search the records of the Immaculate Conception Catholic Church for a record of him, but alas, he disappears into the coal fields forever. I went back down the mountain to resume my original quest for Laurytown. For the life of me, I could not find it. Back and forth across Buck Mountain road I went, until I saw the rustic old Buck Mountain Hotel. I decided to stop in and ask for directions. What a find I came across that day. It was here I met the owner John Strizak. Upon walking into the Buck Mountain Hotel you step back 150 years in time. The barroom is filled with many antiques and artifacts from days gone by. The ceilings are supported by huge wooden, hand-hewn beams. In an anteroom stands a large old stone fireplace, great on cold wintry nights. From the taps at the bar Yuengling Lager flows freely. John and I spent the afternoon reminiscing about the old days of Buck Mountain. He filled me in on much of the history. We spent most of the afternoon in good conversation. John told me a great deal about Buck Mountain.

The Hotel was built by Buck Mountain Coal Company in 1843 and run by William Koons. On the same spot, earlier, stood a log tavern dating back to 1810. Some of the previous owners before John Strizak were the messieurs Ferry, Boyle, Kline, Fiesner, Maurry, and Billy Linski.

Buck Mountain Coal was founded by Asa Lansford Foster, Samuel L. Shoeber, Jacob F. Bunting, Benjamin Kugler and William Richardson in 1836.

During the Civil War, Buck Mountain coal was very much in demand for its clean burning properties. The coal was highly prized by the Union Navy and in great demand as fuel for the Monitor, the iron clad ship that defeated the Confederate Merrimac.

There was no breaker in Buck Mountain and coal had to be transported over the mountain to Rockport. In November 1836, The Buck Mountain Coal Company shipped its first load of coal to Philadelphia via the Lehigh Canal. Coal wagons, hauled a distance of five miles by mules, were later replaced by trains. A 200-foot tunnel was built connecting Buck Mountain and Rockport. The new railroad and the tunnel where both completed in 1840. At Rockport, the coal would not only be sorted and sized, but also cleaned.

In 1875 Buck Mountain's population was over 600 people and consisted of 50 dwellings, a school, shoe manufacture' company stables, post office, general store, and the Buck Mountain Hotel. But like many of the coal towns, Buck Mountain experienced a quick and early demise

My great great grandfather Paddy Brennan came to this area from Ireland in the 1850's. Patrick and his two brothers, James and Frank, boarded at the hotel during their first winter in "Amerikay." They and other single miners slept in shifts at the hotel while in the employ of Buck Mountain Coal Company.

Buck Mountain prospered through the coal years as the industrial revolution took hold in America. Much change was to come to the town over the years. By 1843 the town had one school. In 1880 the population grew to 675. The mines at Buck Mountain closed in 1883 due to the low price of coal and the effort it took to get the coal out. It was then the Coxe brothers bought the village for $22,000. They closed the mines and most of the people moved away.

My ancestor Paddy Brennan moved down to Summit Hill, where I found him in the 1880 census. Summit Hill was where Paddy raised his family. They are all buried in Saint

Figure 1 - Home Scene

Joseph's old cemetery, all except his son Andy Brennan whose grave can be found in the new cemetery out on White Street.

Back at Buck Mountain, John and I said our farewells and I continued on my search for Laurytown. John had given me excellent directions and I found it with little trouble. I was taken back by all the old white wooden crosses marking the poor souls who spent their final days at the county farm and are interred there. Very few of the graves have markings and only God knows who they are. The farm buildings and barns are all gone now. The property is privately owned and has been subdivided into smaller parcels. Laurytown was once a self-sufficient operation housing the county's indigent and infirmed with compassion and love. Poor farms were an idea of the early Quaker settlers. It was their way of caring about their fellow man and their right to the basics of food and shelter at the while same time earning their keep. Times were very hard in the coal region during the last century, but not so cold as to let a family starve in the cold. Unfortunately, many looked at going to the poor farm with shame and disgrace. I was glad to finally find this place. My notes over the past year mentioned it frequently and I had never visited it. I felt a sense of presence having stood on the land where Paddy Brennan spent his final days, and any feeling of humiliation dissipated. It was here on this land I felt completely in touch with the past and the last member of my ancestral family who came over from Ireland at the time of the starvation and blight.

Who were the Molly Maguires?

During the mid-1800's the area of northeastern Pennsylvania was overrun with families from Ireland who had come to the region in search of a new life and a day's work.

They were fleeing the oppression and tyranny of their homeland, Ireland. They had hoped to leave behind in Ireland the hard times, evictions, and starvation they experienced at the hands of the British government. As they began to work and settle down in their new homeland they soon realized the same type of problems existed here at the hands of the American cousins of the royalty that ruled Ireland. In fact, much of America after the Great Revolution was financed by Englishmen. Once again, the Irish were in the hands of English bankers and landlords. Soon, many of the new immigrants found work in the coal mines and quickly discovered mining to be a very dangerous occupation. Too many of them lost their lives to cave-ins, fires, explosions, and horrendous accidents. Often the injured were discharged from employment. They soon realized they were not paid adequately for the hard work and risks they endured.

The miners lived in "toolbox-like" homes — taken out when they were needed for a particular task, and then tossed out on the culm banks when their usefulness ended. The homes were owned by the coal companies and the miners and their families existed at the whim of the local superintendent. The miners were compelled to buy all their goods and needs at the company store at exorbitantly high prices. Items such as tools, necessary for the job, were also a requirement as a condition of employment. The company was permitted to charge whatever rates for these tools it deemed appropriate. Too often, the miner was paid in inflated script that could only be redeemed at the company store, or the cost of his tools was deducted from his paycheck. Many a miner found himself with a bobtail check at the end of the month on payday. All his operating expenses were deducted from his pay — charged against his earnings — and if he was in luck he walked away breaking even. The other

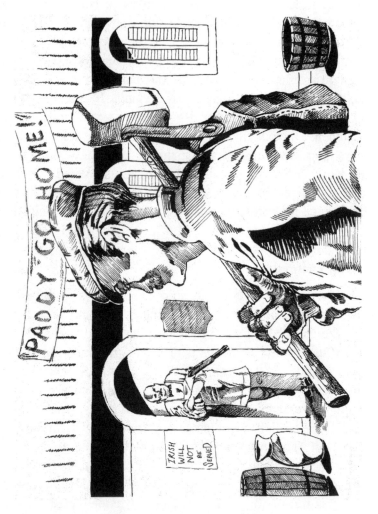

Figure 2 - Paddy Go Home

option a miner often faced was owing the company money on payday. If a miner or any member of his family did business at another independent store he faced being fired. In this way, the coal company constantly kept the miners in debt so they could not quit their jobs and move on. Many miners did manage to slip out in the night to other coal patches where they could start anew. If they were caught too often at this the men were sent to the poor farm and their families left destitute. The wife would end up living with relatives and the children would be farmed out to any relatives that could take care of them.

The railroads owned by many of the larger coal companies controlled life in the coal patches of Schuylkill and Carbon Counties. The most powerful of them was the Philadelphia and Reading Railroad, having combined interests in coal, both mining and transportation of the product.

In the winter of 1873 a coal combination of five companies was formed. In today's terms we would call that a cartel. Franklin Gowen, President of the Reading Railroad, called the major coal companies to a meeting in New York in order to fix the price of coal. Not only were the miners being taken advantage of, but the general public was at the mercy of this cartel and its greed. Coal was fixed at a price of $5 a ton, thus being the first case of price fixing in the United States. As a result, the general public had no sympathy whatsoever for the miners and their plight. Clearly, the miners were blamed for the outrageous price of coal.

The Workers' Benevolent Association, to which most of the miners belonged, had made minor advances in achieving better working conditions and compensation for their toil. Their advances were abruptly halted by the coal operators. In December of 1874 pay was reduce by 20%. Soon after, another

10% cut was levied on the miners. The miners went out on strike for 7 months, only to come crawling back at the demand of the company. Gowen had been informed that the miners were going to strike and he managed to stockpile enough coal to meet the winter's demands.

Many of the men who supported the strike were singled out by the coal operators as troublemakers and would not be called back to work when the strike was over.

In order to gain the support and sympathy of the populace, Gowen was quick to trump up charges that the troubles in the area were cause by a gang of ruffians known as the "Molly Maguires." These men were reported to be a group of terrorists who would stop at nothing to rule the region with tyranny and mayhem. The name "Molly Maguires" was taken from an old legend in Ireland, probably from County Cavan, about a group of men who terrorized the landlords in that region. Molly Maguire allegedly was a woman who had been dispossessed by her landlord when her son came to her aid. The son was very coldly and calculatedly murdered by the agents of the landlord.

In Molly's name the local people rose up against the injustice of the landlord and his agents. The Mollies were blamed for looting, burning, rioting and shooting of the establishment who ruled and deprived their families of basic human rights.

At this time there was no such society known in the United States, but Franklin Gowen made sure to reinvent this organization in order to recoup the sympathy of the citizens then living in the region — German, Welsh and Irish alike. Diabolically, he linked the names of the men who led the efforts of the "Great Strike" to the fictitious organization called the Molly Maguires. Franklin Gowen wanted these men out of his mines and out of the area for good, to be punished and banished forever in the jails of the Commonwealth of Pennsylvania. It was then many of the men became extremely desperate and would cross the line of insanity to achieve their goals of a decent life for their families.

Some of the men known as the Molly Maguires were probably guilty of many of the accused crimes against the state. They had been pushed to the wall and would strike back any way they could. Others were not guilty of any crimes, but suffered the same plight just for being Irish.

In 1873 Mr. Gowen hired thugs from the Alan Pinkerton Detective Agency to infiltrate the coal fields and expose the men who were at the core of all this mayhem. The most infamous of the successful detectives sent in was James McParlan, alias Jamie McKenna. In the three years McParlan was in the area, he gathered and fabricated enough evidence to permanently remove 20 or so innocent Irishmen from their families and friends forever. Among them were John Kehoe and Alec Campbell. These men were both very respectable, educated and influential citizens of the region. They commanded much respect among the local citizens. This was clearly evident by the large number of mourners who attended their funeral. Both Irish and Welsh alike cried out about the injustice levied on these men.

History has proven these men to be completely innocent of the crimes they were charged with, while others who went Scot-free were clearly guilty of their dastardly deeds upon mankind. It was in these evil men that Gowen found solace and retribution. The cruel atmosphere of the anti-Irish prejudice prevented these men from having a fair trial. The men had been pronounced guilty in the newspapers preceding their day in court. The reporting of many of the nation's newspapers called for convictions before the trial even began. The men were not given the right of trial by their peers. Not one Irish Catholic was selected for jury duty. Many of the jurors were illiterate or had formed an opinion from the diatribe printed in the media. As a result of this miscarriage of justice, four accused Mollies met their death in the Carbon County Jail on June 21, 1877, The Day of the Rope, or more commonly know as "Black Thursday."

This was the only time in the history of America that innocent men were hung as a result of a private corporation bringing charges, providing fraudulent information, instigating mayhem, and privately arresting innocent men for their conviction and demise, only to advance the cause of greed and the subjugation of the country's minority and immigrant citizens. The coal barons had set a precedent to follow and issued a warning to anyone else bent on speaking out.

The Mark of Innocence

Much has been written about the handprint on the wall of Cell 17 in what is currently known as "The Old Jail," in Jim Thorpe, Pa. The story goes that a Molly Maguire was hanged proclaiming his innocence and placed his hand on the wall, leaving his indelible handprint to prove his innocence. The earliest written word on the subject goes back to the 1930's when George Korson wrote his book *Minstrels of the Mine Patch*. He states in one chapter that the handprint belonged to Alec Campbell. In another chapter he questions the handprint and its authenticity, claiming it belongs to Thomas Fisher. Prior to that book, no written word exists, only the oral legend and in it arises the name of Alec Campbell. The oral tale comes to us from Campbell's own family in Ireland. A descendant of Alec Campbell named Patrick Campbell wrote the book entitled *A Molly Maguire Story*. In it he recants this legendary tale told many times by his father. So what is the truth about the handprint?

Four Irishmen accused of the murders of John P. Jones and Morgan Powell were railroaded by the Carbon County justice system of the 1870's. They were Alec Campbell, Mickey Doyle, Edward Kelly and John Donohue. They were housed in the cells of Carbon County Prison. Printed in the *Shenandoah Herald* of June 18, 1877 is a diagram of the cell block showing the numbering of the cells. The drawing is made facing the back of the prison, so on the left are cells number 1, 3, 5, 7, 9, 11, and 13. On the opposite side of the cell block are cells number 2, 4, 6, 8, 10, 12, 14, and 16. Cell 14 is where Campbell was located and Cell 7 is where a man named Patrick O'Donnell was being held for a separate trial. Kelly, Doyle and Donohue are being held in cells on the upper level. The current Cell 17, once numbered Cell 7, is where the handprint is located. Does this mean it is the handprint of Patrick O'Donnell and not Fisher or Campbell at all? The answer is no. Patrick was never condemned to die, so he would have no reason to make such a proclamation. He admitted guilt for his deed and served seven years at Eastern State Penitentiary in Philadelphia, Pa.

Thomas Fisher was executed in 1878. He gave a reporter from the *Mauch Chunk Coal Gazette* exclusive rights to interview him and write about his last hours on earth. So we have an accurate telling of Fisher's movements in the hours before his hanging. The Gazette reports that as he was led from his cell to the gallows he was handcuffed, manacled, and shackled in heavy chains. It was physically impossible to reach high on the rear wall of his cell and make the handprint.

The handprint is not that of Thomas Fisher and to say otherwise is only based on speculation and interpretation. It is likely that had Fisher proclaimed his innocence in such a dramatic manner the reporter would have noted it. Since he did report all of Fisher's last thoughts and feelings, it is hard to believe he would leave out something as extraordinary as the handprint.

In the case of Alec Campbell, documented proof that he was actually in that cell does not exist. In Patrick Campbell's book, he states that Alec Campbell stepped out of Cell 17 the morning of the hanging. The *Mauch Chunk Coal Gazette* places him in cell #14, it is on the opposite side of the cell block in the layout from the Shenandoah Herald.

I found one very small but significant paragraph in the Gazette on June 21, 1877. This issue was put out as an "extra" to report the final events of the hanging. Nowhere do they report any occurrence of Campbell placing his hand on any wall and proclaiming his innocence. However, the day before the execution the sheriff moved all of the condemned to the last four cells on the left side of the lower cell block. This places Alec Campbell closer to the actual cell where the mark appears today. Did he leave it? Yes, I truly think so, but I can't prove it. Can anyone else?

There was word of an attack on the jail, and they moved the Mollies around to secure their location within the jail. The sheriff also moved his family out of their quarters in the front of the prison to an unknown location. The Easton Greys, an elite military unit marched up Broadway to the prison and took their places standing guard around it. The Coal and Iron Police patrolled the streets of Mauch Chunk and residents were encouraged to stay home and inside that day until after the hanging. All the taverns were closed that day and all the following weekend.

Is there any scientific proof concerning the handprint? Yes, in 1994 the Department of Forensic Sciences from George Washington University in Washington, D.C. conducted tests and studied the matter. The results of their findings are incomplete due to the limited testing they were permitted to do. They could not definitively say if the handprint was that of Alec Campbell or whether it was made in 1877. The professor wanted to paint the mark, lock the cell and return in a day to see if the mark returned. From the tests they were allowed to conduct this is what they found. First, they took infrared photos under both short- and long-wave ultraviolet light conditions. The handprint was examined under close inspection with several different type of magnifying apparatus. The wall was scanned with a metal detector, looking for any ferrous materials. One very interesting discovery was made. The handprint is that of a left hand and not a right hand as previously believed. This is an important discovery, because all the written material claims that Alec Campbell ground his right hand in the dirt in the cell floor then dragging his ball and chain after him, took a long stride towards the wall, stretching himself to his full height, he smote the wall with his hand. "There is the proof of my words," he said. "That mark of mine will never be wiped out. It will remain there forever to shame the county that is hanging an innocent man." This was reported by George Korson in *Minstrels of the Mine Patch*. Everyone who has written the story since has used his theory and told varying degrees of the same tale. The first time I saw the handprint I thought it was left handed. The mark appears macroscopically and microscopically as a dark smudge on the wall. It has contours and the configuration of a hand print. It is not an imprint or an impression, nor is it a concretion or excrescence from the wall. The matter that made the print has been absorbed into the wall and its underlayment. Under time limitations it was not possible to precisely determine the time date of this handprint or any other date precisely or approximately. When using infrared photography it is clear that brush marks appear on all sides of the handprint. This could mean that in the famous 1960 repainting of the wall with green latex paint really did not occur or that later on there was painting that did not paint over the handprint. The metal detector did not find any metal devices or materials under the wall surfaces. A microsil casting of the wall was unremarkable except that there was a trace of the smudge not observable to the naked eye that got removed with the casting. This indicates that the blackened smudge is literally only skin deep. It is very superficial and not an extrusion from beneath the surface.

The overall opinion of these educated gentleman was there is some considerable doubt the print was placed on the wall in 1877 and that it will re-emerge on its own, without human intervention. There is also the disparity of the Korson story and the right hand print versus the findings showing the handprint is really that of a left hand. There are other scientific techniques available to examine the paint and plaster from the cell wall in a comparative fashion. However, time and money were limiting resources. The simplest test that could be conducted would be to paint over the mark and see if it bleeds through.

At this point the case of the handprint is still an unsolved mystery. Perhaps we should let it remain at that. What we must keep in mind is the handprint is a symbol of the injustice and oppression dealt the Irish citizens of Carbon County in the 1870's.

Death on the Pipeline

The warm sun of Indian summer was high in the morning sky as that infamous day in September dawned. You could feel the rays of heat on the back of your neck long before 7 AM. Humidity had gripped the area all week long as the last picnics of summer came to an end. August's dog days were lingering on as the cool mountain nights grew longer. That was one of the joys of living in this area. The weather might get hot and uncomfortable during the day, but when the sun went down the nights were very cool and comfortable, great sleeping weather. After the long hot summer it was a pleasure to experience the crisp night mountain air. Fall would soon be upon the land and too soon to follow was the bitter cold winter of Carbon County.

Early all that morning groups of miners were traveling from Tamaqua on the New England and Lehigh rail line. The first stop for them was at the depot at Number 3 coal works, where most of the miners and helpers dismounted the cars. Getting an early start meant finishing work before the afternoon sun could bake the mine surface and its workers alive. The men going down in the pit to work would be cool all day long. Mine temperatures beneath the earth were a consistent 50 degrees from summer to winter. The men on the "Lokies" (locomotives) would not only feel the heat of the sun, in contrast they would also have to put up with the hot steam engines they operated. The steam machines provided much of the power used to run the mine operations. Lowering the elevators in the shafts was accomplished by the steam engine. Hauling the "Jimmies" up and down the planes was steam powered. From the steam powered pumps the excess water was pumped out of the deep mine sump holes.

The young boys in the breaker would feel the heat more that any other worker at the colliery. Here they would sit spread legged at an uncomfortable backward angle, sorting coal and picking out the slate or rock that came through the rotating sieve overhead. All around them hung a thick cloud of coal dust. If you looked up at the light streaming through the high mounted windows you could see the filtered particles of silica dancing in the sunlight as beams of light streamed like columns of gold onto the stone coal passing down through the chutes. The boys working in the breaker were as young as 6 years and as old as 15. Here they sat in the heat of summer and the bitter cold of winter, 10 to 12 hours a day. While it was necessary to stay fully covered in winter to stay warm, the same was also required in summer. Staying covered up with thick heavy clothing was a necessary protection.

The blue-black coal dust could penetrate the skin of these very young boys and cause permanent skin irritation and discoloration. The boys wore caps covering their heads to keep the dirt and dust out of their hair, ears and eyes. Over their face many of the boys wore large bandannas to filter the air of harmful carbon and silica particles. The breaker was naturally hot from the intensity of the sun and lack of good ventilation.

At lunch the boys would get to go outside in the fresh air where they would often engage in a game of Gaelic football. Some would just sit and take in the fresh air or walk to a nearby stream and clean the grimy coal debris from their faces. At any rate breaker life was miserable and most boys would anxiously

Figure 3 - Bottom of the Shaft

await the day they could leave the breaker to become a mule driver in the mines.

Climbing the banks of the plane at Number 6 was the water supply line called the "pipeline." This structure was part of the massive aqueduct that brought fresh clean water from the manmade dam at Lake Hauto. Its girth was about eighteen inches in diameter and it ran the entire length of the plane up to Number 6. The underbrush had been cleared by slash and burn techniques, clearing a path to lay the pipeline segments. No vegetation grew along the pipeline as the right of way was oiled down periodically to keep dust devils to a minimum. The right of way held deep ruts and gouges in the land, from erosion caused by the draining mountain water. Without any scrubs growing along the pipeline there wasn't much to absorb the excess run off of rain and melting snow. During torrential downpours runoff from the mountain and the plane created a virtual creek at the pipeline location.

This erosion of earth combined with the intensity of the hot sun and its spiteful rays baked the earth and caused great cracks in the surface of the soil. This made climbing the pipeline to the colliery above an arduous task for anyone taking the short cut from Storm Hill.

John McKeever was out early that day. He was on his way up to the Number 6 breaker. John was the foreman there, in charge of the boys at the breaker. John and his brother James came here from Killkenny, Ireland. They were from the only area in Ireland where deep coal mining was conducted. From their experience in Ireland they gained much of the knowledge that made them valuable coal miners and, proudly, their experience distinguished them from the rest of the Irish laborers. James was working at the Number 9 coal mine. He was the safety inspector at that works. His work day began at five in the morning every day. James was underground at Number 9 that day.

When the McKeever brothers first came here from Ireland they originally settled in Mockanoy City. Later on through membership in the fraternal Ancient Order of the Hiberians (AOH) and friendship with Alec Campbell they came to the coal works at Ashton and Storm Hill.

Alex was working a breast of coal that he leased from Morgan Powell many years ago. He needed two experienced men to take charge and supervise the operation, while he spent his time at the bottling business. He offered the McKeever boys an opportunity to work for him, first at the colliery in Tamaqua, then later on they would all go over to Storm Hill and work the choice coal there.

In the early years after Alex's arrival here, he decided to spend only a few years in the mines. Alex saved every cent he earned and often worked extra hours for additional pay. When he saved enough he bought a saloon in Tamaqua, started its operation and then leased it to his cousin James Carroll.

The town of Ashton was a small Welsh community in full support of the temperance movement. They met at each others house every night in meetings of prayer and song. This method of fellowship was a great comfort during the long strike of '75. As a result of this activity Alex met with much local resistance when he announced he was opening a saloon in the middle of their neighborhood. He became very much disliked in the neighborhood and was often suspected of illegal deeds. Alex was blamed for everything that went wrong in Ashton-Storm Hill. Many of the miners and laborers would stop at his bar on the way home, for a pint to two and discuss the days work in the mine. Very often much union business would be informally conducted in Alex's bar. Soon loose neighborhood gossip of Alex being a Molly Maguire would spread throughout the patch towns in the local area.

One of his enemies in the coal business and a major opponent of the saloon was a man by the name of John P. Jones. He and Alex wrestled over the right to mine coal, but Alex won out. Still grudges were held by both men. Now Jones would try to prevent Alex from earning his living as an inn keeper. While Alex ran a modest saloon and bottling business, he also ran a 10-room boarding house on the floors above the bar. This operation allowed him to employ several family members in the hotel business.

Often local men would come to the bar in the evening and help with the bottling. Alex would pay them a modest sum and all the porter they could drink while bottling the brew. The tavern was an active place of camaraderie and merriment. Miners often stopped there on the way home from work to wash the coal dust from their parched mouths and throats. Before leaving the bar Alex would fill up their copper lunch pails with fresh cool beer or porter. He had quite a thriving business at this location on Storm Hill. The hustle and bustle of the bar trade, the noise late at night and the fights that spilled out into the street was getting on the nerves of the Welsh citizens, especially Mr. Jones who lived a few doors away.

Alex did his best to be a good neighborhood business, but a saloon attracts a certain clientele that God fearing church people can't tolerate. Jones was doing his best to organize a movement that would remove Alex from the block. Alex wasn't phased by all this. He viewed these problems as just normal daily business challenges. Alec was very good at handling these situations. He had power and influence all over the valley and he was viewed as a respectable businessman.

Other Irish miners wanted to do the same for themselves after learning the success Alex had and they came into Alex's saloon for advice about getting their own business going. Very cleverly and carefully Alex would assist them in their pursuit in this endeavor. He would often back them financially or help find a good location to setup business. James Sweeney of Summit Hill was one of those Alex helped to start the Eagle Hotel. James agreed to buy all his beer and porter from Alex. The Irishmen who were successful promised Alex to employ only Irishmen who were put out of work by the Welsh bosses.

The Irish in this community were beginning to gain some economic clout, a move that was felt all the way to Mauch Chunk and the offices of Asa Packer and General Charles Albright. These two men were the eyes and ears of the captains of industry, namely Franklin B. Gowen and Edward C. Clarke, two powerful and wealthy men who controlled the coal fields and railroads.

Gowen was busy buying up land in the coal fields while Clarke was monopolizing the railroad system. Pretty soon, anyone who was involved in the coal industry would have to deal with one or both of these greedy moguls.

One of Gowen's chief aims was to destroy the Working Mens Benevolent Association (WBA) — a union of coal miners, much the way he discredited the leaders of the Bates Union so many years ago. Around 1858, Jack Bates had been framed and accused of stealing funds from the union membership coffers. Gowen had planted a man inside the union that would see this plan come to fruition. Once the Bates Union was banished, the coal owners would command this land as they believed God intended. Edward C. Clarke was the man behind the financial backing and Gowen was the soldier in the field who knew how to destroy a good man's reputation. Packer provided the judicial power to convict those in the sights of Franklin's aim. Their sights were now set on Alex Campbell, the AOH, and the entire membership of the WBA. Gowen saw economic slavery for the Irish as a viable means to profit his operations.

As John McKeever stiffly climbed the pipeline he saw three strangers coming out of the bush in an area just above the train depot. The cars from Tamaqua were unloading passengers when the shots rang out. People were dodging and jumping to the earth as bullets flew about. John, startled by the gunfire, jumped into the brush and crouched down near the edge of the pipeline. From here he could see very clearly who the men were. He did not recognize any of them, but could give a clear description of the three assassins. After John Jones fell to the ground, the trio made their way up the pipeline and passed the wooded area where McKeever was concealed. They did not see him as they spoke in excited tones. In an instant the group disappeared over the mountain. Fast on their heels was a posse of men dogging their trail over Sharp Mountain. John came out from his hiding place and stopped the men to report what he witnessed. John identified one of the killers as looking like a rodent. He said the men were headed for Tamaqua, where they would lay over somewhere and take the cars back to Schuylkill County the next day.

Quickly Constable Davis telegraphed the news to the Tamaqua depot where Issac Haldeman, the telegraph operator, relayed the message to the police; but first he notified Mr. Beard and Mr. Shepp of the vigilance committee. Next step,

Figure 4 - Death on the Pipeline

Davis organized and deputized two more posses to go after the trio of death. One group of men was to take the path to Summit Hill and search for strangers in town. He emphasized checking at the Rising Sun and Sweeney's Saloon, two known hangouts of the Molly Maguires. The other group had instructions to take the short route to Tamaqua, through the great swamp outside the towns of Bull Run and Seek. He had hoped to head off the killers by circumventing their route over the mountain. The initial group had crossed the mountain and were headed out the White Bear way to Owl Creek, hoping to catch up with the killers as they reached the Little Schuylkill River.

Earlier that day over in Mount Laffee, County Schuylkill, two friends, Ed Kelly and Mickey Doyle, were getting ready to look for work in the mines and were prepared to travel as far as Tamaqua, on foot, in that quest. They had spent most of the day going from one patch town to the next. The boys had been involved the big strike of 1875 and supported the union's cause. It was this reason that kept them from getting any work in the mines around St. Claire and Mount Laffee after the strike. All the union miners had been blacklisted from working in the mines of Schuylkill County. The boys were on their way to Carbon County looking for work when they stopped in Tamaqua to rest by the Tamaqua Spring. The cool mountain water was most refreshing to their parched lips as they drank from the pool of gathering water. It was here they decided to rest awhile and cool off. The sun was at its highest point now and causing great discomfort. They took off their dark jackets and hung them on tree branches to air out. Rolling up their long sleeves of their white shirts they splashed cold water on their faces and arms. Here they rested for the afternoon and took a short nap by the cool running stream of the spring.

After about an hour of slumber the boys were awakened by the sound of someone coming through the brush. Not knowing who was approaching, they reached for their pistols. Coming up the road from Tamaqua was a short dusty man who rambled to himself as he walked. He stopped at the spring to wash the dust from his throat and clean his face and hands. Just then the two men came out of the bush with their arms drawn. The stranger in their midst was Jimmy Kerrigan, the notorious brawling Irishman from Tamaqua. Jimmy's reputation was known all over Schuylkill and Carbon County as a short-tempered violent ruffian. He recognized Doyle and Kelly from the AOH picnic in Shenandoah that summer. All three men were loyal members of the AOH. They exchanged secret handshakes and pass words there in the bush. Kerrigan explained he was waiting for two of his friends as they looked for work in the mines. Kelly and Doyle didn't know it then, but Kerrigan was setting them up for a fall. He would implicate the two men in the killing of Jones.

Doyle and Kelly said they were in the same predicament. The trio sat by the spring discussing work and union business for about another hour, when all of a sudden a large group of men descended upon them with clubs and pistols. The Irishmen were taken by surprise and disarmed of their pistols. The group of attackers were the Tamaqua Vigilance Committee comprised of Wallace Guss, Samuel Beard, and Vance Shepp.

Kelly and Doyle were surprised and confounded as to why they were being treated like scoundrels. The only explanation they received was to be quiet and obey the commands. The three were being arrested for the murder of John Jones in Storm Hill earlier that morning.

Back at the Tamaqua jail house Doyle and Kelly gave their explanations why they were in the bush at that time. Kerrigan was treated like a gentleman. Special considerations were afforded him, while Kelly and Doyle were slammed into the lockup. Kerrigan was searched but not detained in a cell as were Kelly and Doyle. Kerrigan said nothing; he was waiting for his opportunity to implicate the two men from Mount Laffee.

Throughout the region the news quickly spread that the murderers of Jones had been captured by the vigilantes in Tamaqua. Mobs were gathering to take the men and lynch them. The police put a heavy guard around the Tamaqua jail that night to protect the trio from vigilante activities. Early the next morning they were transported by a secret train to Mauch Chunk for arraignment and detention in the Carbon County Jail. Their train had to pass through all the small towns of Carbon and Schuylkill Counties, starting at Seek Bull Run, Skintown, Frogtown, Lansford, Nesquehoning, Lausanne, Coalport and Mauch Chunk. Folks mobbed the track along the way trying to get a glimpse of the accused men.

Kelly and Doyle would have separate trials accusing them of the murder of John Jones. Kerrigan would become the surprise informant that would implicate them in the murder. Kerrigan had setup two innocent and unsuspecting Irishmen as part of the plan concocted by McParlan and the detectives.

Kerrigan would never stand trial. He was turned loose for his cooperation in the whole matter; however, he fled the region for his own safety.

In 1909, Kerrigan passed away in Manchester, Virginia. His tombstone reads "James Higgins" and he was interred in a

Protestant cemetery. It has been reported that Kerrigan was afraid of reprisals from Molly families and assumed a new name and identity in Virginia. Repeatedly, he returned to Carbon and Schuylkill Counties to shake down the authorities for witness fees claimed due him for breaking the Molly Maguires.

What really happened the day of the Jones shooting? Well, Kerrigan fit the description to a tee that John McKeever gave of a rodent-like man of short stature acting as the lead or point man, who was involved in the shooting of Jones. John would also state that Kelly and Doyle were definitely not the men accompanying Kerrigan up the pipeline.

As for Kelly and Doyle, they just happened to be hapless dupes in the whole plot. Due their damp clothes, as a result of sweating and bathing at the spring a story was invented by the prosecution of them escaping Ashton over the mountains and crossing the Little Schuylkill River at the South Tamaqua Coal Pockets. The truth is Kerrigan did lead two men on this path, but they escaped out the Lewistown Road beyond Tuscarora and back to Pottsville. Kerrigan took another route through the main parts of Tamaqua to provide an alibi as to his whereabouts.

When he met Kelly and Doyle, at the spring, he was on his way to Reevesdale, to meet with the two assassins that accompanied him earlier that morning. Kelly an Doyle were the perfect patsies. The only crime they committed was being in the wrong place at the wrong time. The law was quick to put an end to this madness and trumped up outrageous charges against the men.

In the end Kelly and Doyle were tried and found guilty of killing Jones. Alex Campbell's name was dragged into the fray because of his disagreements with Jones over the bar he was opening and he too was tried for the murder of not only Jones, but Morgan Powell, who was shot several years earlier. Alex's comment at his trial was "Are ya goin ta hang me twice?"

The real killers slipped away and to this day we don't know who they were. We can only suspect that James McParlan the infamous Pinkerton detective and his band of miscreants were involved in the assassination of Jones.

The end result was 20 men would find their way to the gallows for crimes they did not commit. The AOH would be disbanded and outlawed for a time to come; the union would be broken. Many of the Irish fled the region for their own safety.

It would be the newcomers like the Italians, Poles, Eastern Europeans along with the remaining Irish who would continue the fight, who would listen to the tales of the Molly Maguires and experience the same injustices at the hands of the coal and iron barons. In later years the "Day of the rope" would not be forgotten in the halls of labors' never ending struggles.

In due time, the men of the coal unions would triumph in this war, but not without great costs to the families and men of the United Mine Workers of America.

Today, we find ourselves in a similar situation, working unheard-of hours at arduous jobs that only make the modern day robber barons richer. They care not for our welfare as they strip every safety net we have. Will we as modern day Americans organize and unite in a formidable organization as the United Mine Workers did? Or will we succumb to the business world as we slip deeper into the role of the have nots? Lest we not forget our ancestors and their struggle against tyranny, first in Ireland and then in Pennsylvania at the hands of

English and Welsh oppressors, in the spirit of the Molly Maguires.

A Molly Mysteriously Drowns

The following is an account I came across while scanning old copies of the *Mauch Chunk Democrat* on microfilm at the Dimmick Library in Jim Thorpe. It is a story about an Irishman named Frank Brennan who is mysteriously missing at the time of the County Democratic Convention in Mauch Chunk during the month of September 1876. Not very much was accused of the coal magnates because the State never tried the men on the charges levied. They were tried by the coal corporations, arrested by a private police force, and incarcerated and prosecuted at the expense of men like Asa Packer, Charles Parrish and Edward W. Clarke. The State merely provided the courtroom.

Here was an unimportant Irishman dealt a fatal blow and tossed into the lower Lehigh Dam. Carbon County and its laws didn't care about him very much; they were too busy hanging the Irish. Why bother to find the murderer of one trivial Irishman. Or was he? Oddly enough I found that Frank Brennan's name appeared in the files of the Pinkerton Detective Agency and the summary James McParlan gave to Franklin B. Gowen, president of the Reading Railroad. Was Frank Brennan's death a mishap as the sheriff would have us believe or was it really the dirty work of James McParlan and his phantom brothers still at large in Carbon County? According to the Pinkerton Detective Agency, James McParlan fled the coal region in March of 1876. Curiously enough, the newspaper posted a notice that a letter was waiting for him to claim at the Mauch Chunk Post Office on October the 7th. Was it a payoff, for removing yet another influential Irishman from the list of delegates to the Democratic Convention? In many circles it is believed that McParlan was more of an instigator than an investigator.

Below is the article, verbatim as it appeared in *The Mauch Chunk Democrat,* October 14, 1876.

Found Drowned

It was on Friday the 20th of September that Frank Brennan, a miner employed by the Buck Mountain Coal Company, left home to visit with friends at Summit Hill, in whose company he remained until Monday morning when he came to Mauch Chunk where he attended the Democratic County Convention. While here, he, like, alas, too many others, became intoxicated and when the rest of the Banks Township delegation started homeward, he remained. When last seen on the day in question, it was after dark; he was then alone in one of the saloons, alone but still somewhat intoxicated. When he left, or where he went after that nobody knew. Not returning home on Monday his family and friends grew naturally alarmed, and deputed (i.e., deputized) some persons to come on here to make inquiries concerning him. They did so, but elicited nothing however but that at some time during Monday he had quarreled with several of his acquaintances, which of course at once led them to suspect that Brennan might have been foully dealt with. They returned home and nothing further was done in the matter until Wednesday last when, at the request of his friends, the bottom of the lower dam was dragged in search of his body, and the dragging and grappling had not proceeded long, when Mr. Josiah Harlan, one of the searching party drew his body to the surface. The news of the discovery spread like wild-fire, attracted large assemblage to the spot, and again aroused the suspicion of foul play, which however was partly allayed when it became generally noised about the money that the deceased was known to have had about him, had been found intact. Nevertheless, an inquest and postmortem were held, and the latter not resulting in the discovery of any marks of violence upon the body, the jury simply found that the deceased came to his death by drowning. The two individuals, however, who are said to have quarreled with him on the day in question, were arrested, although no one pretends to claim that any evidence (save the barefact of the quarrel) exists to justify proceedings. At the conclusion of the inquest the remains of the deceased (who leaves a wife and four children) were forwarded to his late home for burial. The general impression here is that Brennan having the occasion to retire, had strayed into the dam.

Judge for yourself what happened that month of September 1876. The men who were reported to be members of the Molly Maguires were lying low, a perfect time for the retribution to occur. Frank Brennan had another brother, Patrick, who upon the news of the murder, fled the County and established a residence at Heckshersville. Years later after the trials were over he would return to Carbon County and take up residence at Summit Hill where he met with an untimely and mysterious explosion in the mines at Number Six. Patrick survived the attempt on his life but was left blind in one eye and partial vision in the other. He lived another twenty years and when he passed away he had been in the care of the Carbon County Poor House at Laurytown. A third Brother James disappeared after the drowning of Frank and was never seen or heard from again.

The Murder of Frank Langdon

In this story I would like to tell you about murder of Frank Langdon and the hanging of Jack Kehoe. These events were relayed to me by Howard T. Crown who along with Mark Major of Pottsville, co-authored a book entitled *A Guide to the Molly Maguires*. The book is an excellent compendium of the events and the players of the Molly Maguire saga. In the book are high-quality, detailed reproductions of the early maps depicting each town involved and great photos of the main characters involved. With this book you can take your leisure with a self guided tour of the region. Howard also runs guided tours of the events and places pertinent to the Molly Maguire period. In his tours he tells a story of the significance of each stop and provides detailed handouts.

Mr. Crown first came across this story while serving his country in the Army at Fort Campbell, Kentucky. The article had to do with the Civil War and the civil unrest on each side during the war. It described an incident at Audenreid, Pa. and the Irish coal miners in the area.

The Meeting

Howard met with the two descendants of Jack Kehoe and Frank Langdon in Girardville, Pa. on the stormy Friday night of June 14th 1996. At a meeting in the historic tavern once owned by "Black Jack Kehoe," reputed king of the Molly Maguires, among a small circle of friends and relatives, two men closed one chapter of the Molly Maguire saga with a firm handshake and warm, heartfelt sentiments.

At 7:03 in the evening of June 14, 1996, Joe Wayne, a Girardville resident and the great grandson of Jack Kehoe, met

Figure 5 - Kehoe Reflections

with John Bugbee, a 48-year-old resident of York County and the great grandson of Frank W. S. Langdon, a murdered mine foreman from Honeybrook in Schuylkill County. They clasped hands and extended warm greetings to each other, thereby culminating an infamous event that occurred 134 years ago.

The murder happened on an extremely humid Saturday night, June 14, 1862 a public meeting was held at the Williams Hotel in Audenreid. The local men were making plans for the fast approaching Fourth of July holiday. At this meeting was Frank Langdon, a ticket boss from the McReary Colliery at Honeybrook; he was the main speaker that night. Langdon also served as Sunday school teacher and one of the events was to be a parade of all the Sunday schools in the area. A recently organized men's coronet band was to provide music and a prize would be awarded to the best marching group.

Mister Langdon had previously secured two American flags from the company store and on this ill-fated evening had led the Honeybrook contingent up Main Street to The Williams Hotel, bearing one of the American parade flags. Marching along beside Frank Langdon and proudly carrying the other American flag was Jack Kehoe, a young Irish coal miner. The two men were close neighbors in the Honeybrook coal patch, living in the same section of the patch.

The American flags were then draped over the hotel porch railing. Langdon and a William Canvin, among others, gave short speeches. Angry words were exchanged between the men on the porch and some of the Irish miners in the crowd. The Irish were resistant to President Lincoln's draft tactics in deliberately singling out the Irish immigrants to fight the Civil War while many native born citizens, of prominence and wealth, were not drafted. One of the speakers accused the Irish miners of cowardice and Un-American activities. As the evening progressed, the meeting ended and the men had adjourned to the tavern located in the hotel. Langdon's friends noted his absence and started a search. William Canvin walked south, past Hamburgers stable and down Tamaqua Street to Bach's Hotel. After not locating his friend, he went to Honeybrook. Still unable to locate Frank Langdon, Canvin returned to The Williams Hotel where he found his old friend badly beaten and lying on a table in the tavern's kitchen. Doctor Demming arrived from Jeansville to heal the badly beaten man.

Very early the next morning some friends helped Mr. Langdon back to his home in the patch at Honeybrook. Despite the doctors best efforts, Langdon passed away two days later. Before his death, he stated to his friends that he had not recognized any of his assailants.

Other than the County Coroner's inquest, no action was taken until fourteen years later. Then, in the frenzied environment produced by the Molly Maguire trials and fever, "Black Jack Kehoe" and several others were charged with the murder of Frank Langdon.

Neil Dougherty and John Campbell preceded Jack Kehoe to trial and were found guilty of second degree murder and sentenced to 20 years each. Kehoe went on trial in Pottsville, January 9th, 1877. At the swift three-day trial, he was found guilty of first degree murder. Jack Kehoe was hanged in December of 1878 after all appeals to the County and Governor Hardtranft were exhausted.

There the matter has rested until today when the two descendants met for the first time. John Bugbee explained his connection to Langdon and related to the small group his family's experiences since that fateful day 134 years ago. Joe

Wayne likewise made the small gathering aware of the struggle to survive on the Kehoe side.

Maria Andreas Langdon raised her son and daughter by teaching for several years at the school in Honeybrook. When her son was old enough he went to work in the same mine his father had worked. Mrs. Langdon continued to live in Honeybrook until her death in 1891. She is buried beside her husband at St. Johns Lutheran Cemetery.

Mary Anne Kehoe continued to operate the tavern and hotel that Jack Kehoe had operated in Girardville. The property and estate was passed along to her daughter Mary Ann and on to Mary Anne's daughter, Alice Wayne, a grand lady of some 90 years, who still lives at the hotel.

It was in the early morning hours when the meeting came to an end, coming full circle on a relationship which was shattered by the events on that fateful evening of June 14th 1862 in Audenreid, Pa. Both men expressed their hope that the healing can continue.

Clergyman "Knocks" Hibernians

The following is a brief article I found in the *Mauch Chunk Democrat* from Saturday January 11, 1908. It concerns one aspect of the legend of the Molly Maguires. The item is about Father McDermott who was a chief aid and bedfellow to Franklin Gowen and his gang of warlords during the prosecution of the men and women from Carbon and Schuylkill counties in the late 1870's. While he gave the last rites to his fledglings he also testified against them in a court of law, sometimes bearing false witness.

When this article appeared it was some 40 years later after the hanging of the 20 men from the two counties. You can see Father McDermott still has no more compassion for his flock than he did in 1877 on "Black Thursday." In one sentence he refers to the church as "his church," then later on threatens to go public with what he claims to know about the men called the Molly Maguires. Strangely enough he never did expose them, because there was nothing at all to tell that would damage the men of Erin. Father McDermott was spewing out his own brand of fire and brimstone once again, just as he did from the pulpit in Pottsville when he denounced the AOH and excommunicated AOH members with the reading of Archbishop Wood's pastoral letter. Isn't in interesting that the establishment side of the struggle all fared very well for themselves. Father McDermott got a nice parish in Philadelphia and the coal and iron company donated prime acreage to the church for the construction of the seminary. The sons of Erin played right in to their hands when Gowen was brought on board to break up the union organizing efforts.

I am very glad to see the revitalization of the AOH and its gaining respect as a true fraternal organization to promote goodness and charity amongst its members, something the Church of the 1870's knew little about. Here is the article; read for yourself and decide.

Dateline Philadelphia January 11, 1908

Members of the Ancient Order of Hibernians were greatly stirred up by the refusal of reverend D. I. McDermott, rector of St. Mary's Roman Catholic Church in this city, to permit funeral services to be held in his church over the remains of John Daly, a parishioner, because a Hibernians Lodge had been invited to attend the obsequies. Because of Father

McDermott's opposition to the Hibernians the funeral had to be postponed. Subsequently the invitations to the Ancient Order of Hibernians to attend the funeral was revoked, and the funeral was held from the church.

Father Mc Dermott in an explanation of his opposition to the society said he formed an opinion of the Hibernians during the Molly Maguire reign of terror in the Pennsylvania coal fields. He said: "My absolute opposition to the Ancient Order of Hibernians is based on my knowledge and facts in my possession about the Molly Maguires which I got from the condemned Molly Maguires themselves. No power on earth will ever make me recede one inch from my stand against the Hibernians. I have given testimony against them and what I said was true and is true and I cannot compromise on it. Archbishop Ryan and a number of other prominent clergymen are aware the facts I have in my possession against the AOH are true and that if made known will cause the greatest kind of scandal. I have a mind to give them to the public."

Those secret files, Father McDermott spoke of, now lie in the cellar at the St. Charles Seminary on the Main Line in Philadelphia. I wonder with the revealing of those documents who would truly be scandalized, Father McDermott, Franklin B. Gowen, the Church or the Molly Maguires.

Poems

Summit Hill

From the depths of my childhood memory there's a place that I recall

As the days of my existence approach September

Summit Hill, Summit Hill, the town where I was born

I remember the streets of coal and the fields at Tampico

Down through Stony Lonesome and over the meadows of Bloomingdale

Out White Bear Way and Sharp Pinnacle

Summit Hill, Summit Hill a place I cannot forget

Once titled the Township of Penn in Towamensing.

A site where the Indian villages once flourished in the valley of Mahoning.

Twas' sparsely settled common where few English did reside.

Ginther and coal brought the Irish and the Welsh.

Deep mining and the Switchback were the tools they used.

Over Sharp Mountain to the Planes at Number 1.

Bringing down the coal to breaker Number 6.

Then the folks of Erin came to make this place their home

From places like Donegal, Galway, Cavan, and Meath

Summit Hill, Summit Hill, their home in this the new land.

Of the many names that sounded, Breslin, O'Donnell, and Kane

Brennan, Boyle and the families of the Lamb

Soon too came the Kings of Killishandra from far beyond the sea

Summit Hill, Summit Hill calls out to me

Surmounting Panther Valley she stands like a citadel on the hill

Remembering the lazy days of summer, running down the paths
of town.

Through the streets of Hazards to the cemeteries at White.

To the burning mine that made the grass ever green

Along Railroad Street where Morgan once fell.

And finally I can taste the water in the well.

Down by McMurtrie's tree

I remember all of this very well

Summit Hill ... Summit Hill ....Summit Hill...

The Poetry of Mickey Doyle

Found in the Mauch Chunk Coal Gazette *from July 14, 1877.*

Prisoners as long as we are innocent.

And our conscience light and free,

Will trust in God and be content,

With whatever his will may be.

But still alas! I cannot rest,

While my parents they do sigh;

I pray that God will them bless,

And grant them heaven when they die.

Ever since we being imprisoned,

It has caused their hearts to grieve,

And they done their whole endeavors

To obtain their son's relief.

Great heavenly Father, the star of light,

Pray comfort them each day,

And lift their souls upright

When they are called away.

Where could you find better parents than mine

Who has proved themselves to be,

Who stood to me through thick and thin,

To regain my liberty.

It has pierced my feelings so severe,

And the heart starts in my breast,

To think that I am the cause

Of their troubles and distress.

"The Exiles Farewell"

It was on a summer evening, it happened to be.

That I took the notion to cross the stormy sea.

I said unto my Father and my friends, both one and all.

"Soon I must good-bye to you say and leave old Donegal."

It's of a gallant ship I heard lately that sailed away.

With many an Irish exile bound for America.

And when she does return again it is the last for me.

For to set sail in the evening gale to the great land o' the free.

Farewell to all my loving friends in dear old Massinass.

Twas there I spent my childhood days, "Ah but now Alas."

But I am growing older and I must go away.

And leave my dear native home. I can no longer stay.

No more through Ard's green woods, I'll roam at noon or even-tide.

Or wonder by the Cloon stream which was my joy and pride.

Or watch the foaming breakers of Thramore, so wild and grand.

Or see the fishers cast the nets along the Castle Strand.

Farewell to all my comrade girls and one above them all.

And twice farewell to my own dear home, in the wilds of Donegal.

My eyes are filled with tears, my heart is sore with pain.

For God knows if we ever meet in Erin isle again.

Adieu, Adieu, fond heart so true, the hour is not far.

When upon Creeslough town with all around, I'll step upon the car.

My gallant ship lies awaiting, the foule for to sail down.

Farewell, farewell I am now away from dear old Creesborough town.

It was on a graceful morning the day I went away.

With comrades true along with me all ready for the sway.

And at old Hassey's garden where darling hearts beat sore.

I said farewell and waved my hand. I could say no more.

We quickly passed through Barne's gap and gazing all around.

I took one look on Doon Rock where O'Donnells chiefs were crowned.

I thought upon the days of old and of brave Caher Roe.

And how we met and nobly fought at ancient Castle Doe.

It was early the next evening from old Erin we did part.

I thought that the day at Derry quay would surely break my heart.

And sailing in the tender I did cry my fill.

To see the big ship waiting for us down at Novill.

With a captain too and a jolly crew that night we sailed away.

And in the morning early we were far upon the sea.

For light long days on board that till one morning I did see.

The wood and near and the hills are clear of the great land of the free.

I seen the lofty mansions and the towering mansions grand.

I have seen the flag of freedom wave over that foreign land.

I have seen the Irish exiles that came both one and all.

To welcome here their own dear friends that came from Donegal.

For away from Donegal and Cushla gal ma chree.

But when I earn a fortune, I will return again.

My back I'll steer to Erins isle across the stormy main.

But yet please God the day will dawn that old Ireland will be
free.

And keep her sons and daughters fair from wandering over the
sea.

And give them peace and plenty and pleasures too galorah.

Oh-gramma-chree I long to see sweet Erin og astoragh.

Composed and written by Bridget Kelly

Michael Doyle's Saint Paddy's Day Poem

Doyle's St. Patrick's Day Poem.

It was early on this morning,

As on my bunk I did sleep;

I was awakened by the brass bands

Playing on the street

So I did rise and rub my eyes,

No more this day to sleep;

And when I thought the day it was,

I jumped up to my feet.

Saying can I walk or can I talk,

Or can I anyone see? No!

But closed up in a dismal cell

In hopes of Liberty.

And when I came to myself,

And in my cell did hear

The music that the band did play,

It gave me good cheer.

And when the tune was finished,

And the band it ceased to play,

I passed remark upon myself,

And on them, these words did say:

But shortly after that,

before a half hour passed,

 The turnkey he came in,

And gave me my breakfast.

Can I walk or can I talk,

Or can I anyone see? No!

But his one thing I can do

Is to eat my grub pretty free.

When he was about to go,

After I got my coffee and bread;

I spoke some words to him

And these are the words I said:

So then I sat down,

My breakfast for to eat,

For, when a man is in good health,

I tell you it goes sweet.

Now to conclude and finish,

With one more thing to say,

This is a nice way to be.

Stories

On Saint Patrick's Day!

Having spent some time in the Carbon County Prison on a winters day I can feel the pain, sorrow and anger that Michael is experiencing as he takes his pen in hand. The cells of Carbon County are cold like steel on a February day and deathly damp enough to chill you to the bone. The only light in the cell is that which comes through an angular slit in the wall, also letting in the cold air from above. While a beam of light shines on the cell room floor one cannot see the sky outside or the birds taking flight into the air. Constantly, all you can hear is the clanking of the guards' keys accompanied by the swinging wooden doors and iron grates. You hope is that someone is coming for you to bring the mail or a chance to walk out in the yard.

There is no escape from this hell hole. Repeatedly, they move everyone around from cell to cell to avert a rescue and you hope they don't move you to the dungeon floor. For here on the lowest level not even the sun shines through the slit in the wall. Here you lie on a cold stone floor with only some straw for a bed. Through the cave darkness one has to grope for the chamber pot and hope it doesn't spill over. The rats and the centipedes are your only company throughout the day and the night. Even the deepest darkest coal mine is not this bad and you hope you don't die here tonight.

After the evening meal of stale bread and potatoes the turnkey gives you a candle to keep the night. The warmth of the flame brightens your soul before it too soon flickers out to an ember in the dark.

It is then the ghosts of this old dark castle come to haunt the night and torment your sleep that doesn't come all through the night. As the candle finally extinguishes itself a rotting stench slides from under the door. You know who is with you now as your stomach turns over and you wretch you bowel. Even the rats have left you to the one's who own the night. It is now that you realize the devil has come for your soul. Will you last the night? Part of you wants to but the other hopes you die! Another night in this dungeon you will never want to try.

In the morning they move you again, hopefully it's back upstairs to the dull light and cold damp air. Day in day out this is the life you have. At one point you will agree to plead guilty even if you are not. Anything to get out of here even to swing free against the background of the sky.

The only pleasure you experience is that rough wooden bowl of hot black coffee that will come in the morning at first light. Over its warmth you will thaw out your bones and down your gizzard take in the heat. One more night have your survived this torture and torment and all anybody wants is to see it end as you hang from the rope. Soon enough they will get their day for what you have to say means nothing now. Your fate is sealed by the hands of the coal companies justice.

Michael spent another Saint Patrick's day here in the jail before he hung from the gallows, on June 21st 1877, just outside the cell where he spent his final days. The next day he was packed in ice and carried away to Mount Laffee for burial.

Turnkey Madara was instructed to clean out his cell where found several of Michael's poems. Thanks to Mr. Madara we have insight into Michael's last thoughts. In fact, in spite of his frightening experiences, he managed to have only sweet thoughts of his last days on earth.

The poem was written especially for Turnkey Madara in thanks of his considerate treatment at the hands of his oppressor.

Me Old Grandfar

When I was a wee bit of a lad, me family lived in Tamaqua, Pennsylvania. Twas' a small coal town on the dusty floor of Panther Valley, in Schuylkill County. Me family had lived here for generations; in fact, they settled in this area at the time of An Gorta Mor, the great Irish hunger. Me folks were simple but hard working miners, scratching out a bare existence from the rich carbon deposits buried deep in the hills of the Sharp Mountain. This hard life brought about hardships and heartbreak stories that all coal crackers and their families share.

We are gone far away from that time and place now, but I remember the tales handed down to us from Granfar about the ghost of the old miner. His yarns were always amusing as bedtime stories on those bitter cold winter nights, in the dark wilderness of Panther Valley. One of the interesting things about Grandfar's musings was the places he spoke about existed in the streets and neighborhoods of our little town. You could go out the next day and check out for yourself about the places he talked about.

The story of the old miner was about an innocent man, hung for the murder of another man he barely knew. The miner became a legend to the working class in the valley who remained there after his demise. Many other miners had skedaddled out of the region to save their necks from the coarse feel of the rope. The old miner had stood up to the coal companies in the region. He advised the men who worked the hell pits below about their rights as free Americans and kept up the heritage of strong Irishmen. Alas, he met his death, but not in vain. He and 19 other martyred lives were the spark that ignited the entire valley into organization of the mine workers. Irish, Welsh, Italians, and Slovaks all joined the union of miners that had been struggling to stay alive o'er these last 30 years.

The night I came in contact with the spirit of the old miner, I will never forget. Twas' Halloween night Friday October 31st of 1947. My sister Audrey and I were with a group of kids coming back from the downtown business district. The merchants of town always offered their store windows for the painting of Halloween scenes on mischief night and Halloween. We were climbing the iron steps at Nescopec Street as a heavy fog rolled into the area. The top of the steps took us to the foot of St. Jerome's old cemetery. Twas' always a challenge to walk through the old burial place on Halloween night. We could have just as easily walked around the bone yard and down the wooden steps on the other side of the hill by Vangelder Street to Spruce and quickly home.

The group stood there arguing who was going to go in first, as we did the fog grew more intense, making the challenge additionally frightening. By the time it was decided all would enter together the fog had thickened to a pea soup. One could barely see 10 feet out in front. Gingerly we all climbed the old concrete steps to the cemetery.

In the fog, we had lost our way, when we came upon a man standing by a tall monument. His face was blackened and he wore an old dark three-quarter length suit coat. He sported a short dark beard of whiskers from his chin and a bushy salt and pepper mustache. He spoke no words or made any sounds, but seemed to just float over the mist covering the earth among the stone markers of the deceased Irish settlers. His hat sat askew on his head exposing a red mark that appeared to be a wine stain birthmark. Upon his feet he displayed heavy leather boots. The sight of him caused the girls in our group to scream aloud an run off. Only I was left standing by the man as he looked out over me. My feet were frozen to the frosty earth and I couldn't move from the fright within. From outside the yard some of the other kids were yelling me name. I was petrified and the cat had taken me tongue, as Granfar would say.

The macabre figure reached out to me and touched me shoulder. I was shaking like a branch in the wind. His arm touched me and the two of us levitated over the fallen stones and markers of St. Jerome's Cemetery that night. He took me on a tour showing me the plots of his friends. At each name we paused and settled to the ground. First there was Ellen McAllister, then Friday O'Donnell. The last name I recall was Columbus McGee. It was here we paused the longest. The miner seemed to fill up with sad emotion. Sharply his head turned and looked down at me. What a puny sight I must have been. There I stood wet in my pants and shaking from the cold. I felt like I was about to be eaten alive right in that spot. Quickly he dispatched me to the edge of the cemetery were I entered earlier that night. I had reached an opening in the fence and my sister and friends were all waiting outside. Suddenly I had touched down the earth again and stepped out of the cemetery. Sheepishly I turned to see if the man was still there. I no longer saw him. Just then out in the street I saw my sister. She was yelling and was furious with me. Audrey thought I was playing one of my usual tricks on her. We were late for getting home and Ma would kill her. Angrily she stormed toward me with a bramble in her hand. I was about to be beaten in her rage. Startled with fright, she stopped dead in her tracks a few steps from where I stood. Her eyes opened wide with utter terror. She told me to quickly jump down the steps to her. I felt something warm on the back of me neck and turned to see what it was. The stranger dressed in old clothes stood visible behind me. He reached out to touch my shoulder again with his warmth. Audrey fainted to the ground. Rapidly she gained consciousness as me Ma and Pa approached us from the street. In the flick of a light the stranger disappeared. Our parents and others had been worried about us, they gathered together in a group to search for us. We were several hours late arriving home. Me Daa came up the step to pick me up at the top of the cemetery and carried me away. Me poor sister got a scoldin' for keeping me out so late. All of us went home and never again spoke of this night. A few years ago while passing through town I stopped the car and walked along the side street by the old cemetery. It was all grown over with weeds and high grass now. Many of the tombstones had fallen down and it was in much disrepair. The church had removed the old wrought Iron fence from around the yard and constructed a chain link fence around it with a locked gate. I paused at the base of the disintegrating concrete steps, were I once stood that cold October night 50 years ago. Everything came back to me in a flash. The steps were no longer of much help climbing the small hill entering the yard, so I had to struggle a bit. When I reached the top and viewed over the fence, only one very large tombstone was clearly visible. On it read the name John Kehoe. Below his name was the inscription: "A native of the County

Wilklow, IRELAND. Died December 18, 1878. Aged 41 years, 5 months, 15 days." Just then an icy cold chill came over me, cooling the warm summer day. Night was falling and back to my hotel I was bound. Later that night as I sat in the pub in Summit Hill telling my story, everyone sat spellbound. When the evening ended I realized the events of the day had prompted me to drink a bit too much porter. I was feeling the effects of it now. The barroom was closed and only one old gent remained behind. He brought over one final pint for us and then he sat and told me of a similar story he witnessed as a boy growing up in Tamaqua. We had shared the same experience. It's been years now since I last saw the old man; he has passed away. The old gentleman was me Granfar and, yes, he and I both experienced the spirit of the Molly Maguires and the spectre of "Black Jack Kehoe."

Wolf and Prey

The wind whips in from the Potomac making the canyon lined streets of town feel like frozen valleys of the Alaskan Tundra. Icicles hung from the ledges of magnificent gray-toned multi-story buildings so dangerously close to the ground. Pedestrians had to walk at the extreme edges of the sidewalks, almost to the point of stepping into the streets and competing with the passing horse-drawn carriages. The place is Washington D.C., the nation's Capitol, the time is early December 1889, just a few short weeks before Christmas.

Commerce and government business are heatedly conducted here daily on a twenty-four hour schedule. Greedy men meet in dimly lit back rooms or in smoke filled taverns. They trade their souls for large, quickly made fortunes. This is a story of one such man who traded his soul away so many years ago in the black coal fields of northeastern Pennsylvania. For the story's sake we'll call him the *Prey*. This is also a tale of another man we shall call the *Wolf*. The wolf stalks the murderer of his kin and countrymen, damning his own soul for eternity with the blood of his victim. The two of them, wolf and prey, walk the pavement of Washington going about their business. Remarkably, the two men look very much alike in physical appearance and stature. They could be brothers, as they are dressed like a proud mother would dress her twin sons. The two men are not twins nor are they related, but fate will bring them together on this frigid day.

The wolf is a poor Irishman, who came to this country to learn the business of being a slave in the coal mines of Carbon County. He is alone in this world after having lost his sons in the same dark dungeons he spent his miserable life digging out the black diamonds for the robber barons in Schuylkill and Carbon counties. His wife died during childbirth in their home one bitterly cold night. The shanty they lived in had only a pot bellied coal stove for heat. The coals had burned out and the young mother laid alone on a bed of straw on the rough hewn floorboards. Her husband and sons were at the mines on night shift. Neighbors came in the early morning hours to look in on her and found her and the new born child both frozen to death. In later years he lost each son to the hazards of the mine. Alone now the wolf was destined for the almshouse and a life of further servitude in abject poverty. Wolf had snapped and could take no more, he vowed he would take down the man who raped and pillaged his world and anyone else who got in the way.

The prey is also an Irishman. He is born to the privileged life of the ruling class in this new land of America. He was born on his mother's private estate in Mount Airy, a well-to-do suburb of Philadelphia, educated in the finest schools of Maryland and Pennsylvania. He enters the business world at the top and quickly rises higher. Not satisfied with the wealth he has accumulated he begins to hunt and starve out the laboring inhabitants of this harsh land, gobbling up coal lands in one purchase after another.

A cartel is formed by the prey and his cohorts who intend to rule the Anthracite world. The workers in the fields try to unite and form various benevolent associations to protect themselves from the wrath of the English bankers and their cruel American cousins. The cartel plans to break the miners and bring them to their knees through a life of indebtedness and servitude working for the company. A great conspiracy is concocted by the cartel and a trap is sprung on the miners. In 1878, twenty of them pay the price for unity and defiance of the coal barons' cartel.

Having been successful in his endeavors the prey now moves on to bigger conquests. In Washington he now finds himself a mover and a shaker in the world of big business, commerce and international financial matters. From the buildings of the Commerce Commission this gentleman, dressed in his warm reefing jacket and fur lined hat, wanders down the back alleys taking a short cut to his hotel. Upon reaching Wormleys Hotel he exchanges pleasantries with acquaintances in the lobby. A quick trip to the hotel bar, with his good friend Major Stevens for a nip of brandy on this cold day. Later he'll go to his room and pour over the legal contracts and matters involved in his latest scheme, crushing the Southern Railroad.

The wolf makes his way through the old streets of Georgetown to an area where no one will ask his name or his business. He finds the shop of a gunsmith and steps inside where he haggles with the proprietor over a battered old army pistol. He pays what appears to be an exorbitant amount for the pistol and promptly dispatches himself from the shop. Armed with this instrument of death he walks into a local Catholic church to administer his own last rites of his conscience. Staying for about an hour in church he prays for the lost souls of his family and vows to take vengeance upon their oppressor.

Back out on the street he walks briskly uptown towards Wormleys Hotel. He has practiced this march often and perfected his impersonation of the prey so well that most general acquaintances cannot tell the difference between the two men. In this manner he has gained the confidence to penetrate the hotel security and go unnoticed to the room where the lawyer is working on his important contracts.

The lawyer decides to go down to the hotel restaurant for a quick bite to eat. Shortly after he leaves his room the wolf gains entrance using a homemade key. In the corner he waits for an hour until the lawyer returns. He inserts the key in the lock and pauses as he realizes the door is unlocked. Fatigued as he is, he thought leaving the door open was his own mistake.

Entering the room he is attacked from behind and the heavy cover of an army coat is thrown over his head. The attacker holds him in a strong one-armed grip, presses the army pistol against his head and pulls the trigger. The body falls to the floor in a pool of blood. Dropping the pistol, the attacker heads for the window and descends three floors down the fire escape. He makes a clean getaway and is never seen again.

The next morning the chamber maid becomes alarmed when she can't gain access to the room for cleaning and summons the hotel manager. The two of them find a man lying dead in a huge pool of clotted blood. The police are sent for and the body is taken away. The crime scene is carelessly trashed by police officers and hotel personnel in and out of the room. Important evidence has been destroyed and there is no way anyone will ever discover who the assassin was. Washington police call the murder a suicide and close the case. The wolf is last seen boarding a train for Philadelphia.

Dateline Washington D.C. December 14, 1889 the headline reads:

Franklin B. Gowen found dead in his hotel room

The ex-president of the Reading Railroad commits suicide!

Family, friends and colleagues are all shocked in hearing of Mr. Gowen's suicide. No one can believe it. His daughter admits her father was having excruciating head pains while on a recent trip to Europe. Dr. Darrach, the family physician, is unaware of this illness. All agree Gowen was a strong and brave man who would never commit such an act. His pastor is totally at a loss for words over the matter. No one believes in the suicide theory, except Captain Robert Linden. He outwardly professes the suicide theory, but in the shadows of Washington's late night he has dispatched several of his detectives to run checks on the recent releases of suspected Molly Maguires who have been released from the penitentiary in Philadelphia. The detectives are all out on this assignment, diligently tracking their men.

Epilogue:

Inside a small tavern at Tuscarora, three wide-eyed Irishmen meet to discuss lodge business with the recent Washington traveler concerning the report of Gowen's suicide. One of them remarks: "To bad his last shot wasn't his first."

They all laugh and toast to a clean job well done, contemplating who is next on the list. The traveler jests, "Perhaps it was the ghost of Molly Maguire." Exit the wolf.

Good-bye My Old Friend

The streets of this great country haven't exactly been paved with gold for me. Leaving Ireland when I did, and under certain circumstances, has cast me into a sea of despair and despondency from the moment I set foot in this cursed land. This place is run by the bastard American cousins of the Brits that I left behind in Erin. There is no place in the land to seek refuge and solace. A day's pay for a day's work is all I ask. Between the Welshmen and the Roundheads a days work gets me hide skinned to the bone. I have drifted from one patch to another seeking out honest work and have asked only to be left alone. The life dealt to me is that of one boarding house after another, one hell pit deeper and darker than the last, only to be wiped out on payday by the company store. It's no wonder me brothers have turned to the one method of advancement the English understand — Violence! It may not be an answer but it surely is a voice to be reckoned with.

With these thoughts in mind I packed me bags one more time and headed further west into the Schuylkill coal pockets and over the mountain to Columbia County. In coming over on the cars from a place called Tamaqua, I learned of the great excitement in Bloomsburg that day. It concerned the execution of a man named Patrick Hester. I first met him in the area at one of the conventions in Mahanoy City. I had been following his cause in the papers from time to time as I moved around the coal fields. The idea of this man being brought up on the charges listed was beyond my comprehension. He was a fine man and a good citizen. He was my friend in this difficult country. How could he have fallen to this state I don't know. So it was with some great interest I made my way to Bloomsburg and the foreboding fortress on the hill.

The newspapers claimed my friend was the mastermind in the assassination of Alexander Rea, a murder that happened some 10 years earlier on the Mount Carmel to Centralia Turnpike. Tis' a road I have traveled much myself only to fend off the highwaymen that infest this artery.

Rea was the colliery superintendent at Locust Mountain who had been creating a stir among the miners there by encouraging the practice of short-loading and claiming much of their load was filled with slate and debris. This was a common practice held by the men who controlled the mines, especially leveled upon the Irish miners and laborers.

It wasn't curiosity that made me want to travel to Bloomsburg that cold day in March. I was rather concerned with the welfare of me old friend Pat Hester. There was much hope in my heart that I would see him again if only to bid him a fond farewell. On the train over I discovered the town was under heavy military guard against any purported rescue attempt that had been planned by the Molly Maguires. Upon my arrival I was quickly informed that no one without a pass would be permitted entrance to the jail.

The crowd that gathered there that day was filled with tension and excitement. Police and soldiers occupied the square at all points considered to be vulnerable. Across the street, coming out of Maley's Saloon was a man I met while on the road. I called over to him. He was an old friend of many years from kicking around this wounded landscape; Whorley Hoyt was his name. He had a pass permitting him to enter the prison.

The guards promptly separated us as I had none. Whorley yelled out to me and pointed to the cemetery on the hill overlooking the prison. He was trying to tell me I could clearly view the drama from that vantage point.

The cemetery was just across the street from the old high school and the gallows could readily be seen from this spot. Standing very near me were two very fine gentlemen with a spyglass discussing the finer pints of a hanging. Their conversation appalled my sensibilities. The one man remarked that he had a pass that would gain him entry, but he just couldn't stomach the stench of the filthy crowd and their bizarre thirst for blood. This was the opportunity I was waiting for. I struck up a polite conversation with them about the tragedy that was about to befall the three Mollies. When the one man learned that I was a personal friend of Pat Hester's he generously offered his pass to me. As I left the hill the men wished me well and regards to Mr. Hester, for they too knew him to be a man of good character and standing in the community.

At the jail door I displayed my pass as the guards looked at me suspiciously. I was in, but still had two more levels of guards to pass. At the final checkpoint the one guard slammed me against the wall and two others drew their Winfields on me. The captain of the guards came over and examined my pass. He knew I wasn't the gentleman whose name was on the pass and he asked what I was doing with the pass. I told him how I came about receiving the pass. Just then Dr. Little, the celebrated physician from Berwick, came by and vouched for my integrity. I had worked for him once while in Berwick. For an entire winter I was the caretaker at his office building, before I decided to move on.

Dr. Little took me over to his party of official witnesses and asked if I would join them. We were stationed very close to the gallows. I'll never forget the shock I felt when Pat Hester stepped up on the gallows flooring. He was a large handsome man, about 260 pounds of raw-boned Irishman as I ever remembered him. He was a very distinguished looking man, more like a bishop than an ordinary man. He wore a fine suit of wool. In his shirt bosom he sported a diamond stick pin through his cravat. On his wrist he wore diamonds also. I often wondered, was he really wearing diamonds or was the sparkle a sign of his innocence that gave the sparkling shimmer of diamonds?

Patrick Tully, Peter McHugh and Pat Hester took their place on the gallows footing. Pat glanced once my way. He gestured his recognition of my presence. The hangman's noose was slowly being placed over their heads as Pat stared at the yard office. He was sure that Governor Hartranft would come through with his reprieve in the nick of time. Out of the guard house came Captain Peeler with a telegram, he read it aloud to the crowd. There would be no stay of execution; their appeals had fallen on deaf ears. Pat Hester's facial expression then became very sullen. His lips turned a coal blue and his eyes were lifted up to the heavens. In an ironic twist of fate, Manus Cull, who admitted his participation, was pardoned by the good Governor for his testimony.

Slowly the trio moved into quiet prayer as Father Bunce climbed the gallows steps to say the last rites over the three men. Now the white hoods graced the looks on their faces as they were drawn over their heads. McHugh murmured a few words, which I couldn't understand. Another in the crowd closer to McHugh said he wished he had listened to his "mither" in Ireland. Pat Tully went to pieces on the scaffold causing the hangman to prematurely drop the floor below them. Over 120 persons witnessed the hanging. Many of them cried out loud and sobbed miserably at the sight of the trio falling to their death. Many looked away at the moment of release. A few men actually wretched their guts out at the sight of the men swinging in the breeze. Pat Tully died instantly without a murmur. Pat Hester and Peter McHugh struggled mercifully and clung to their last gasps of breath. McHugh almost climbed the rope he was hanging from as his back arched up highly up on the rope he was suspended from.

The ordeal was over. I was sickened, but at the same time glad I got to see my old friend Pat Hester once again before he departed this life. He almost seemed pleased to see me standing in the crowd. Colonel Harvey and Frank Rhoads were taking the bodies down from the gallows and had called to the men in the crowd for some help. I rushed over to carry down my old friend and gently placed him in the freshly filled iced coffin and delivered him to the family waiting in the yard.

After all the funerals were settled and all me good friends were laying in their graves, I packed me bags and left the coal region for another purpose. I would see that the man responsible for the hanging of over twenty of me countrymen would pay dearly for his deeds. From Bloomsburg I caught the train to Pottsville, where I changed cars for the tracks leading to Philadelphia. At the Broad Street station in Philadelphia I engaged a train for Washington D.C. to where I would seek out the offices of Franklin P. Gowen at Wormleys Hotel. By evenings' end the world would reel in shock at the news of his mysterious suicide. Soon I would be back in Tuscarora planning my next move.

Whenever there is an injustice committed upon an Irishman a Molly Maguire will be there to extract fairness. When Mollies no longer exist the sons of Molly Maguire will seek justice and vengeance. In the end when they are gone the spirit of Molly Maguire will live on.

Murder by Moonlight

There was much to be excited about on that cold winter evening December the 2nd of 1871. The children at St. Joseph's school had just finished their first term in the new school under the guidance of Miss Rose Brogan. Miss Rose had arrived earlier the summer before from the town of Ardara, County Donegal, Ireland. She was only 19, and one of the prettiest lasses to arrive at Summit Hill from Ireland in a long time. Rosie was staying at Summit Hill with the Brennan family, also from Ardara. Rosie was one of the first young women to teach elementary education classes in all of the coal region. The task of school instruction had always been the responsibility of the local minister, usually in a public or Protestant school setting. The Irish Catholics of Summit Hill had decided to form their own school at St. Joseph's Parish, under the leadership of Father James Ward, and teach Catholic education and instruction. The parishioners sent for Rose to come and teach in their town. She was one of the best and brightest minds ever educated in France. On this particular night Miss Rose was in Mr. Williamsons store buying some cloth to make costumes for the upcoming Christmas pageant that was being presented at the church school on Christmas Eve.

Saturday December 2nd was also payday for the miners of Panther Valley. The pay train had just rolled through the towns of Ashton and Storm Hill earlier that afternoon. Mr.

Figure 6 - A strip mine operating at the present time near Shenandoah.

**Figure 7 - The Panther Valley name lives on in this
modern bus company.**

Wiliamson had stayed open a little later than usual at night for late shoppers. Many of the townsfolk were milling around the town square where Williamson had his general store. Working in the store were Mr. Williamson and his young stockboy Jack O'Donnell. They were refilling the shelves and serving customers. Gathered around the old potbellied stove were several men engaged in quiet conversation. Two men were sitting at a small table playing a friendly game of dominoes. In the corner of the store Old Paddy Brennan sat tuning up his fiddle. He would often come uptown on these special Saturday nights and play for the people who gathered in the store.

Above the door to the store was a small brass bell suspended on a shiny coiled steel spring. Whenever anyone entered the store it would ring automatically, to get Mr. Williamsons attention and he or young Jack O'Donnell would greet them at the counter. Some folks just came in to get out of the cold and chat with their neighbors. The store was very much the social center of the small shopping district, in the heart of town. Further down the street was the town hall, which very much resembled the Bastille in Paris. Next to that was the Rising Sun Hotel and Saloon, a very popular watering hole on a Saturday night. Out on the village green stood the Switchback Railroad Depot. Adjacent to the depot were the stables of Mr. Klotz. Down the street was the coal works of Number 6 and the Number 1 inclined plane, which carried coal cars to and from the old mine. The rigging works of the old rail system rose high above the main street of town was called Railroad Street, then Back Street and is now known as Ludlow.

So now the stage is set for the drama about to unfold. In the shadows outside the store, three men had gathered in the cold night air to plot the murder of Morgan Powell. Morgan was the local mine superintendent who was much hated by the Irish for the discriminatory hiring practice he employed at the coal works all over the valley. The media of the time would have you believe Morgan was a much loved benefactor. The truth be known he was rather antagonistic to all his Irish employees who were Catholic and members of the AOH.

Within the confines of his labor practice Morgan very much encouraged hostile behavior towards the Irish Catholics under his charge. Not only were they denied work, he saw to it the Irishmen would not be hired within a 50 mile radius — "blacklisted" was the term. Men who were blacklisted could not find work any place in the region. Whether or not he deserved to die for this action is another matter. Morgan did not give much thought to the miners he starved out and the families he broke up as a result of his callousness, and had total disregard for the Irish miners. The reason he didn't care for the Irish was because he was Welsh and the Welsh were in power, outnumbering the Irish in many patches and most other towns in Carbon and Schuylkill counties. Who was there to stand up for the Irish coal miners?

Enter the AOH, the WBA and the Molly Maguires. The methods to settle disputes in the mines were handled by the WBA first, along with the influence of the much-respected members of the AOH. When all other efforts were exhausted, in stepped the Molly Maguires and their unorthodox tactics of force and violence. The latter was their only the tactic of last resort. Still, all hope was lost when this was agreed upon, as the only avenue of recourse. It was then the organization turned to tough-hardened men like "Yellow Jack Donohoe" who had a sure way of dealing with ornery mine bosses. He often presented them with offers they couldn't refuse.

Earlier that day a contingent of coal miners had arrived in town for a weekend of carousing and merrymaking. The men were all from the mining camps up in Buck Mountain, at the upper most edge of Carbon County. Once a month on payday, the men from the mining camp came to the towns of Ashton, Storm Hill, Mauch Chunk and Summit Hill to let off steam. The town was filled with strangers from the high reaches of Carbon County's wilderness camps. All day long down at Sweeney's Saloon there were fights and arguments, as the drunken miners dispensed their pay and vented their pent-up inhibitions through consumption of massive pints of porter and brandy. It was one of those days when the gentler people of town knew better and tended to stay indoors and off the streets of town. The town had but one constable and he was busy all day long dragging the intoxicated men to the holding cells at the old Bastille. Several times that day gunshots were heard coming from the various saloons of town. There was no law and order as we know it today and Summit Hill was a wide open mining town complete with saloons and brothels. It was a scene out of the Old West, but it was northeastern Pennsylvania in the 1870's.

So on this day it was not uncommon for one to hear gunshots coming from any part of town. Evening had come quickly that day and the darkness seemed to calm and quiet the miners. The people of Summit Hill were a resilient array of hardy pioneer stock. Their cousins were fending off wild Indians out on the central plains of America while they were taming the wild Irishmen in the hills of Pocono country. So a few dozen drunken miners whooping it up in town that night was not a problem.

The crowd at Williamsons store had thinned out to a small group. John Berion was in the store talking to Henry

Williamson about the escapades of Brigham Young, out in the West. Sam Allen had come in to buy tobacco for his pipe and he was waiting for Morgan Powell to stop by with the pay records of the week. The two men were working late that night finalizing the payroll that had just been expended that morning. Money was flowing all over in town, especially at the saloons and brothels. Miss Rose was still looking over the choices of material for the Christmas costumes when Morgan Powell came into the store. His young son, Charles had come in with him. Although Charles was not Catholic he knew Miss Rose very well. Immediately he went over to see her. Miss Rose had a keen fondness for all the kids in town whether they were Catholic or not. Their wasn't a lad in town who could resist her charm. She genuinely had their best interest at heart and cared for them all as her pupils.

Rose now moved over to the counter to complete her purchases. Charles had focused his attention on the penny candy glass cases, mesmerized like only a kid would be. Morgan had abruptly left the store to run over to the offices of the Lehigh Coal and Navigation Company. He cautioned Charles to stay in the store until his return. Charles said he would and then agreed to accompany Miss Rose home safely when his dad returned. All agreed to this arrangement.

Morgan was barely out of the store a minute, when four shots rang out. Everyone thought it strange to hear the gunfire this late at night as the miners had quieted down and most were now sleeping it off in boarding houses. Sam Allen walked over to the large window to look outside when a bullet came crashing through the windows above and just missed him, violently shattering the kerosene light overhead. The round had sent flaming oil out of its vessel, spreading fire all over the floor of the store. Mr. Williamson rushed over to put out the fire that had begun. Panic and excitement spread confusion in the small store.

Moments before the round came through the window, Paddy Brennan had finished playing his Irish ditty. Very carefully he was returning the fiddle to its case. He paused and looked upward with his head turned at an angle to catch the sound of something familiar. Paddy was blind, but his sense of hearing was very sharp. He could virtually hear a pin drop in the dirt from 50 paces away. It was that kind of sound that startled him yet did not surprise him. Moments before Morgan Powell left the store Paddy warned, "Morgan, take care tonight." Morgan stopped and pondered curiously at Paddy. Pat didn't say it then but he heard the cock of a pistol outside in the dark. He quickly put it out of his mind, thinking it was the imagination an old Scot. Years before in the mines Paddy had been blinded by a mysterious explosives accident while working at Number 9. Morgan was mine boss there and was the first to come to Paddy's rescue. After his healing and loss of only one eye, he was deemed satisfactory to work in the chutes at breaker Number 6. Paddy had developed a keen touch for the coal and slate. Paddy never worked in the mine again. While many of the boys suffered from "red tips" as a result of the sharp slate pieces, old blind Paddy could gingerly pluck the sharp objects away from the sound pieces of anthracite. This made him a valuable worker in the breakers. He felt productive and useful. Paddy's sense of hearing was ever that much sharper than his touch. Seconds before the report of the pistol sounded, Paddy heard the projectile pierce the flesh and bones of Morgan Powell. He heard Morgan fall and gasp out for help.

As the others in the store were getting up after ducking flying broken glass and stray bullets, Paddy said, "Boys,

Morgan's been shot." Doctor Thompson had been coming up the street when he saw three men descend on Morgan. Before he could understand what was happening, the flash of the pistols bleached the dark night with streaks of fire. He witnessed three men rush up the rigging stand of Number 1 plane and disappear in the veil of night. Momentarily his attention was taken by the small fire in Williamsons store. The doctor burst through the front door announcing Morgan was shot and lay on the tracks of the Switchback. Sam Allen dropped his pipe as he ran out the door to assist Morgan. He called for the others in the store to follow. Miss Rose grabbed Charles Powell and held him back from witnessing his dad in this condition. Groups of men had gathered in the street and formed a posse to track down the men who shot Powell.

Mr. Williamson ran to the store room for blankets and pillows. Quickly he created a bed for Morgan on top of his counter. Miss Rose brought out whiskey and bandages for Morgan. The best Dr. Thompson could do for Morgan was make him comfortable. The bullet had entered his right front rib and lodged itself in the spinal column. Morphine was the drug of choice for pain then and Morgan was doped up beyond feeling and consciousness. He knew he was going to die and it was important to know who shot him. Morgan had no idea what had happened to him let alone that he was shot. Squire Minnick had been called to the scene of the shooting by neighbors who saw three shadowy figures ascend the planes of Number 1. Dr. Thompson and Miss Rose attended to Morgan all night long as he drifted in and out of consciousness. They both took turns watching after him while the other one cat napped in the store room. Somewhere around five in the morning of Sunday December 3rd Squire Minnick returned with pen and paper. Dr. Thompson was on watch and had dozed off.

Figure 8 - Culm banks are prominent on the mountainside near Nesquehoning, Pa.

Figure 9 - The former home of the McAllister family at Wiggan's Patch near Shenandoah. Ellen McAllister and her brother-in-law, Charles O'Donnell, were slain here by unknown assailants in 1875.

Miss Rose was lightly sleeping in the store room. Morgan was stirring making some sense now. Minnick sat beside Morgan and conversed with him. The Squire felt that Morgan had gained some sense again and began to question him at length. Morgan had recalled that the one man looked like a miner known as "Blue Pat" and another like Kilday. Hastily Minnick wrote up a statement swearing that Morgan had identified Patrick Breslin (Blue Pat) and Patrick Kilday as two of his assailants. While all were asleep Minnick tried to get Powell to sign the paper, but Morgan would not. In a desperate attempt Minnick signed Powell's name and asked Morgan to just touch the pen. Morgan would not! Dr. Thompson has just awakened from his own loud snoring. The sound startled Minnick and he tried to escape the store with the document. Later in court he would claim Morgan signed it and indeed touched the pen, making it all very legal. It was only through the testimony of Miss Rose and Dr. Thompson that the case against Breslin and Kilday was dropped by the State. Their testimony greatly conflicted with that of Squire Minnick. The State realized it had no case against the two men and exonerated them. Early Monday morning the 4th of December 1871 Morgan Powell passed away.

In the months and years following the shooting several other men would be brought up on charges and held responsible for Morgan's murder. Among them were John Malloy, Patrick O'Donnell and Alec Campbell.

The final accusation of the charge would be levied upon Alec Campbell and he would hang for the murder also. Squire Minnich would become the Burgess of town and Doctor Thompson would attend to another dying man (John P. Jones) a few short years later in a place called Lansford. Henry Williamsons store burned to the ground one night and he would move away to Camden, New Jersey. Young Jack O'Donnell was killed by a fall of coal in the Jeddo Mine around 1896. Miss Rose married a handsome young Army officer and moved to Fort Madison, Iowa. Sam Allen would testify at Alec's trial in his behalf. John Berion died from a gunshot wound while guarding Number 6. No assailant was ever found. Old Paddy Brennan went completely blind and would die in his sleep at Laurytown, the county poor house. Young Charles Powell would be brought up by John Berion

Only Alec Campbell's memory lives as the innocent man accused of multiple murders he never committed. His grave lies silently unmarked known only to those who care about his innocence and memory. Alec's handprint remains on the wall of his cell at the Carbon County Jail as a testimony to his innocence. Every year thousands of tourist gaze at the mark of Alec's hand and ponder what it was like to be Irish, Catholic and a miner in the decade of the 1870's

Escape from Mauch Chunk

High atop the Nesquehoning Mountain begins a trickle of water the Indians once called the "serpent providing drainage to the mountain crests." It is the main stream that creates the Mauch Chunk Creek. As the serpent sweeps down the hillside toward the town it joins other tributaries and rivulets all coming together at the top of Broadway, Mauch Chunk's main street. Once all the streams come together at the great pond, the force of Mauch Chunk Creek has reached is most powerful juncture. The creek streams down the hill that becomes the main part of the town. In the early days Mauch Chunk was called Coalville and in Revolutionary times it was known as the Spruce Swamp.

Figure 10 - An ornate stained glass skylight in the roof of the Jim Thorpe Courthouse.

Figure 11- The Serpent (Iroquis Indian name). A swift flowing stream coming down the mountainside into Jim Thorpe.

On its downward spiral through the town, the creek crosses the main thoroughfare twice before it rolls down the steep incline of Race Street. At Race Street it is covered with huge slabs of trap rock and slate thus creating a sluice for the waterwheels of the wire mill it powers at the lower part of town. Once as it passes over the huge wheels of the mill the creek is expelled into the great Lehigh River creating freshets among the rocks as the Lehigh winds its way Southeast to Easton and joins the waterway at the Delaware Canal. From there the canal streams south to New Hope, Bristol and Philadelphia. The Mauch Chunk Creek has been both a blessing and a curse to the town. In times of torrential downpours its waters have often created floods devastating the dwellings and lives of the village at the bottom of the gorge. In good times it has brought prosperity and wealth to the citizens and settlers to the area.

In the late 1860's, when the construction of the prison was taking place, many parts of the creek were covered over just as they were at Race Street. At the site chosen for the prison the creek came dangerously close to the foundation. The engineers decided to place a collection reservoir and reroute the creek away from the prison walls. In the lower part of the town construction had begun to cover the creek at the two points it crossed Broadway. The engineers in this wilderness had conquered the force of this mighty stream at least for the time being.

Lawrence Mulherron came to this country from Donegal with many of the "Famine Irish." He made his home in Mauch Chunk where many were employed at the wire mill, coal yard, river locks, and construction of the new prison. Lawrence was a laborer in the prison project. He worked with the local stone mason Nathan Whetstone. The building was progressing as the surrounding prison yard walls were put into place. Lawrence was working deep in the foundation of what would become the dungeon. It was here the creek passed very close to the southeast corner of the foundation. As Lawrence worked there he could hear the rushing sound of the covered stream 20 feet away. This problem had become a real concern to the engineers and builders. Everyone involved felt the shoring up of the culvert with an additional three feet of granite would be a sufficient method to protect the prison foundation. The county commissioners were anxious to get the prison finished. They threatened penalties on the builder if he didn't complete the project in time.

Most of the laborers on the project lodged at the American House on a weekly basis. The American had one of the best taverns within a hotel. This made it a very popular place to lodge. After a long hard day's work the men would gather in the tavern and discuss the day's construction progress. They were all concerned about the culvert running too close to the foundation corner. It had become a serious problem for the builder. He was cutting corners in the construction in order to pay for the additional shoring of the culvert. Two of the men were talking about it one day at lunch. The foreman overheard them and told them to be quiet about the construction disorders. Later that night they were again discussing the problem and the foreman overheard their conversation. When they reported to work the next day he discharged them and sent them away from Mauch Chunk escorted by Sheriff Raudenbusch. At the edge of town the men were put on a coal barge heading toward Easton and threatened with their lives never to return to Mauch Chunk. The prison was finished on time early in the year 1871 and it was hailed a great

Figure 12 - The Devil's Pulpit, a rock formation near Jim Thorpe. The
Blue Mountain Devil could lurk in woods like this!

Figure 13 - The clock tower of Jim Thorpe (Mauch Chunk)
Courthouse. Note the steep wooded mountainside rising straight up
from the community.

Figure 14 - A railroad bridge over the Lehigh River at Weissport, PA.

Figure 15 - A remnant of the Switchback Railroad at Summit Hill.

achievement in building construction techniques. The new Carbon County Prison was modeled after the Eastern State Penitentiary in Philadelphia. It was considered to be the best and newest in penal confinement. The prison was ready for its first inhabitants by July of 1871.

Mauch Chunk is the main shipping port in Panther Valley, collecting coal mined at the mine shafts in towns like Hacklebernie, Summit Hill, Centerville, Seek, Bull Run, Skintown, Andrewsville, Buck Run, Ashton, and Storm Hill. A unique gravity railroad system was constructed by two founding settlers named White and Hazard. It began in Mauch Chunk at the planes of Mount Pisgah. At the top of Mount Pisgah, on the peak, was placed an engine house powered by steam. Streaming out from the engine house was a huge stainless steel band of metal plates riveted together looping down the entire length of the inclined plane. At the depot the band was attached to a Barney car used to push a coal car up the plane until it passed through the engine house. Once through the engine house the car was released to glide down the slope on the other side of Mount Pisgah, across a high trestle, and onto the flats of Bloomingdale Valley. The next ascent was up Mount Jefferson via the same method as at Mount Pisgah. The coal cars would once again be released to descend the slope of Mount Jefferson into the mining town of Summit Hill. This method was used for many years to transport coal from the mines to the coal chutes and loading docks on the Lehigh River and canal system at Mauch Chunk. The rail system was called the Switchback Railroad. In later years the railroad would break through the Hauto Tunnel and Nesquehoning Tunnel providing a clear path to the docks at Mauch Chunk and direct routes by train to New York and Philadelphia. The Switchback no longer remained an efficient and cost effective way to ship coal. In 1870 it was turned over to passenger travel and remained very popular until the late 1930's.

The burning mine in Summit Hill became a popular sight to see. During a turbulent summer storm in 1859, lightning struck a grove of trees placed near the edge of the open pit mine. The downpour of rain collected about the trees and swept down the hill to the coal mine quarry. The flood washed the burning trees into the deep mine pit setting fire to the rich vein of Anthracite. All attempts to extinguish the fire in the pit were in vain. It burned for the next 60 years until the seam of coal was exhausted.

The Switchback was the main way to get to Summit Hill. The town became a popular mountain resort as a result of the burning mine. The sulfur baths at Summit Hill were thought to be of therapeutic value. A large boardwalk or observation platform was placed at the end of town so visitors could safely view the beautiful glow of the hot coals burning in the open quarry pit. The view was especially romantic at night as the flames danced over coals in colors of green, yellow, red and blue. Hotels and spas were built all over town with a view of the mine from the best rooms. Only Niagara Falls gathered more tourists in those early years of leisure travel. Summit Hill was a prosperous town due to the mining headquarters placed there and the attraction of the burning coal mine. Life in Summit Hill was good. It was always known as a peaceful town until December 2, 1871 when Morgan Powell, a prominent citizen, was shot on the main street in full view of 20 citizens. The men who performed the dastardly deed fled over Sharpe Mountain to a clean getaway. A posse had been formed to track down the shooters, but they were on the wrong trail. The trio of assassins turned west at the Breslin farm and headed down the mountain to Owl Creek Road. The posse turned east at the farm and over Sharpe Mountain towards the great swamp in Tamaqua.

Manus Brennan had just finished a days work at Elias Brenckman's sawmill in Owl Creek and was walking home as he approached the great oak tree located within a half a mile of the Breslin farm. He sat down to rest a bit, when he heard voices and footsteps coming down the slope. Manus' first thought was they might be highwaymen so he crawled into the trunk of the great oak tree and shimmied up the wide shaft. The men stopped right at the tree and paused a moment in their flight. There were three of them, one very short man they called Jimmer. The middle sized man was called by the name "Darcy." He appeared to be just a boy the same age as Manus. The larger of the three men was called Mickey. He was a burly, gruff old-timer, built like a bear. They spent a few minutes changing hats and removing disguises of fake chin whiskers and eyeglasses. Manus held his breath the whole time he hid in the tree, fearing the men would hear him. Mickey decided that since his pistol dealt the final blow he would hide the pistol in the trunk of the tree for safe keeping, in case they were apprehended on the road to Tamaqua. The others did the same. Manus thought he would be discovered as their hands came within inches of his head and arms. Suddenly the sound of barking dogs could be heard off in the distance. The band feared capture and rapidly fled the area. Unknown to them the barking sounds were coming from over the mountain. The acoustic properties of cold night air caused the sounds to carry a great distance. When the trio was gone Manus crawled out of the tree trunk and groped in the dark night for the weapons placed in the tree as he hid there. He could not find all three of the guns. Two of the pistols must have been very small derringer types, falling in to the rotting sawdust of the decaying tree. The pistol he found was a

Navy revolver, still smelling of the cordite from the spent gun powder. He slipped the pistol in the belt around his waist and continued towards his home in Summit Hill. The weapon still had a warm feel from the explosion that propelled the round into Morgan Powell's spine.

Manus was anxious to find the constable and Squire Minnick to tell them what he knew. He was the only man who could identify the killers. Upon his approach to the town center he was tackled by two roughs who were part of the posse. When they found the pistol in his belt, still smelling of having been recently fired, they were sure the killer had been captured. Manus was handled very roughly and taken to the lockup were he would be questioned by the authorities. Constable Painter and Squire Minnick did not believe the story of the men that Manus saw. Later on Manus would be taken to Williamsons general store for a positive identification. Morgan had gained some semblance of consciousness and was sitting up as Miss Rose, the local school teacher, attended to his wounds. Morgan's eyes fell upon Manus and he lifted his hand to point. Just then he passed out from the shock of the wound. The Squire claimed Morgan was about to positively identify Manus as the shooter. Morgan never did regain consciousness and died the following Monday morning.

Manus was booked and held over for trial. Miss Rose and Dr. Thompson protested that Morgan said nothing that would connect Manus with the murder.

The constable was holding the pistol taken from Manus as evidence. The bullet removed from Morgan at the autopsy would reveal it came from the same gun Manus was carrying. A case of murder was charged against Manus Brennan for killing Morgan Powell. He was bound over for trial and held in the

Mauch Chunk Jail. During the trial Dr. Thompson would testify that Morgan never identified Manus as his killer. Miss Rose, Father Magorien, and Mr. Williamson would testify as to the good character of Manus Brennan. The story Manus had to tell fell on the very deaf ears of the court. Manus was found guilty and held for sentencing. He filed an appeal but was denied justice by the tribunal Appellate Court of Carbon County. Justice was not swift or fair in Mauch Chunk for an Irishman during the 1870's. Manus sat in jail for months as his trial and appeal were waged. The sentencing phase of his trial came in the month of May, when Manus was sentenced to be executed by hanging on June 11, 1872. He was returned to his cell at the jail.

The Warden feared that Manus was one of those "Buckshots," a group of militant Irishmen, and had Manus locked up in the dungeon of the jail. He was not allowed any visitors. The Warden was much afraid of a rescue attempt and he took all precautions against it. The jailer tossed Manus into the dark, damp musty cell in the lower solitaire block of the jail. The stench of the cellar was enough to make one retch violently. Manus felt his way around the 6 by 8 cell until he found the pile of straw on the floor that was to be his bed. He had been stripped of all his clothing and left naked in this 50 degree cell. The warmth of the straw on his feet caused Manus to fall to the floor and wrap himself in the straw. The heat within the decaying straw was very comforting and it removed the bone chilling agony of the "Broadway Bastille." Quickly he fell asleep from the effects of the cold floor. He was going into a mild state of hypothermia. Several hours later after a long deep sleep Manus was awakened by a sharp pain in his right hand. A rat had been ferociously gnawing at his finger tips. His hand throbbed with excruciating pain as the adrenaline surged through his body and he could actually see in this darkened cave. A huge Norway rat sat on his chest watching a smaller brown rat chew on the fingers. In a quick move with one hand Manus swatted the vermin off his chest and tossed it across the cell floor. His other hand was throbbing with pain as he grabbed at the beast eating his fingertips. Manus strangled it in one sharp movement. He beat the rat's head on the stone floor to insure it was dead. His attention then focused on the larger rat and its whereabouts in the cell. It was gone! His eyes clearly adjusted to the cave darkness now, he scanned the floor of the cell. Gone! Where did it go? Manus wished he could escape that quickly too! Shivering from the cold of the mountain night he crouched in the straw, gathering his own warmth, he laid there curled up in the fetal position. In the morning the jailer awakened Manus for a breakfast of hot black coffee and bread with honey spread on it. Sitting there devouring the meal he felt no longer alone in the cell. Sure enough, the huge Norway rat sat on its haunches over in the far corner. In the dark the rats eyes shone with a evil glow of tiny green slits, disappearing as the rat would close its eyes. Little did Manus know that this rat would help free the soul.

Early in the afternoon the jailer came again and asked Manus to step out of the cell. Two large blue uniformed guards with repeating rifles stood over him. They led Manus up the stairs to the upper level where outfitting in the prison uniform was done and Manus got a hot soapy bath. He was fed a delicious warm lunch and treated very kindly. The warden called for Manus to come to the main office where he was read the riot act and told he would have to earn the privileges of living in the upper level. Until that time Manus would dwell in the bowels of the Broadway Bastille. Shortly after his indoctrination he was issued some flint and a very small oil lamp much like the one coal miners wore on top of their hats. He would be charged for the oil consumed and the payment would come from any earnings incurred around the jail. Everyone had daily tasks to perform to earn their keep.

Much later that day Manus lit the oil lamp just before his evening meal came. He managed to feel some comfort and warmth from the glow of the bright yellow-orange flickering flame. The guard brought hot stew that night and black coffee. All this was served with a moldy sourdough roll and a large portion of butter. Such a feast! As Manus ate he felt the eyes of that rodent on him. He looked up and sure enough there was the rat staring back at him. Manus tossed the rat a piece of the foul bread. The rat watched it fall on the floor in front of where he sat. He looked up at Manus as if to say, "What's that? Big deal you toss me your garbage!." The rodent didn't move an inch, he just sat there watching Manus. When Manus finished his hot coffee he looked to the corner for the rat. It was gone and so was the bread! Manus thought to himself what a beggar the rat was and decided it needed a name. All that evening Manus lay in the hay feeling warmed by the glow of his tiny oil lamp. He amused himself in a mental game of naming the rat. Immediately he named it after his lawyer "Kalbfus." Naw, that's not fair! Then he thought about "Minnick" — nope, not good either. How about "Packer Rat?" It still didn't jell. Then it came to him! "Franklin B." — that was perfect!

In the wee hours of haunting, Franklin B. came to the cell again. This time Manus was ready for him and waited for the appearance of his rodent friend. Franklin squeezed out of a hole no larger that an inch in measurement. It was almost as if the rat was appearing out of nowhere. The rat wandered the cell aimlessly looking for scraps of food. With nothing to be found

Franklin B. slipped through the tiny hole again. When he was gone Manus quickly crawled over to the spot where the hole in the floor was. It was too dark to see anything, but he could hear a strange sound. What was it? Water! Water gurgling in a stream of some sort. The old Mauch Chunk Creek carved through the underground rock and dirt to the foundation of the jail. Franklin B. was a sewer rat! The rodent could come and go at will in total freedom.

Manus was assigned to kitchen duty as a way to earn his keep. The chores were long and hard. At the end of every night he was returned to his cell without even an acknowledgment. On this night he came back to the cell with a large spoon and a knife, smuggled out of the kitchen. He would have to act quickly. He discovered the entire underlayment in the corner of his cell was made of a soft concrete. The condensation from under the foundation had rotted and loosened much of the mortar and rock composition that made up the floor base.

Quietly he spent the long night chipping away at the soft concrete. It was easier than he ever imagined. After several hours of work much of the cell floor actually started to cave in. Clearly the stream from the creek could be seen now by the illumination of his small miners oil lamp. The opening was now wide enough for a man to squeeze through. It was now or never! Gently Manus lowered himself into the cavernous opening. Downward and downward he slid until he saw Franklin B. He saw the rat immediately scurrying away from him going forward through the tunnel. Manus followed behind crawling slowly one knee in front of the other. He came to a large opening under the main street. The Mauch Chunk Creek streamed by swiftly below. Soon he thought the guard would be bringing breakfast to the cell. It was a temptation to go back, but they might discover the large hole in the cell floor. It was now or never! Manus jumped down into the rapidly flowing creek and rode out the rapids. It was like a wild ride on a raging river or down the chutes of a log flume. In a few short minutes he passed under West Broadway and into the mill race at Race St. The landing at the Lehigh and freedom was not far away!

Although the flow of the creek was rather rapid, when it reached the wheels of the mill, the channel was widened causing the flow force to diminish. The wheels of the old wire mill were not turning, being locked in position for the night. This enabled Manus to slip out of the sluice at the point of entry. He gingerly climbed down the wheel works to the stream below. The waterway was no more than ankle deep at this point. Manus silently slipped away to freedom from Mauch Chunk that night.

Farther down the Lehigh River, in Easton where the Lehigh meets the Delaware via an intricate system of canals, Manus boarded a coal barge that would take him to the small inland seaport town of Bristol. Here he stayed with relatives until he recovered from his ordeal and the heat of his escape cooled down. From Bristol Manus would journey to Philadelphia where he would eventually board an ocean going vessel as stowaway in the hold of a steamer going back to England. Once in England it was a short voyage back to the homeland of Erin. After a four-week, land and foot journey across Ireland Manus found himself back in Donegal. Ardara never looked so good.

Manus was back in his homeland, where the news of his escape arrived before he did; his family was very glad to see him again. When he left Ireland they held a three-day American wake to mourn his departing. It was typical when the first son left home to emigrate across the sea to throw a triple-day celebration called an "American Wake." Most likely, the parents would never see the lad again and it was a proper way of saying good-bye to him forever. The "Wake" was a grand party of celebration going on around the clock until it was time to go. Then the wailing began as the women would see the lad off to the train depot or down to the seaport. But now the prodigal son had arrived home. It was like the jubilation of a resurrection. Never would Manus forget his life and experience in the coal fields of Pennsylvania.

He was safe here in the wilds of Donegal and would live out his life well into his nineties before he passed on, but Manus did escape the gallows of Carbon County.

Six years later 10 Irish Catholics branded as Molly Maguires would hang for similar crimes for which they were not guilty. One of them was for the murder of Morgan Powell; and again, an innocent Irishman by the name of Alec Campbell would die on the gallows for a crime he had no part in committing. It seems that the roundheads of Carbon County were bound and determined to hang all the Irish Catholics on trumped up charges in kangaroo courts.

The townsfolk of Mauch Chunk would forget the young innocent Irishman who made good his escape from the Broadway Bastille. The story was never told until now. The county authorities kept a tight lid on the subject of the fissure in the Mauch Chunk Creek culvert. They figured that in enough time the problem would be fixed. The news and importance of the fissure was quieted as stop-gap measures were taken to tame the wild stream.

Across from the Victorian-style train depot at the foot of Race Street is a steep hill that climbs to the point where the creek crosses under West Broadway. The first building you pass going up the hill is St. Mark's Church where part of the culbvert is anchored into the hillside above. Adjacent to the door of the church you can hear the sound of the creek babbling as it passes under Race Street. Higher up on Race Street is a row of beautiful stone houses once used to house the wire mill workers and supervisors. Nowadays they are shops and a restaurant. Still further up Race Street is an old building now used as a boutique where through an open drain, one can actually see the raging creek roll under the thoroughfare. Whenever I am in town and pass by that way, it brings back to mind the story of Manus Brennan and his escape that day long ago.

Of Past Times

I sat in a hot stuffy court room that Friday afternoon, August 28, 1876. Katie and me daughter Bridgie sat with me. We had lunched in the hotel across the street, where one too many stouts passed my lips. I was feeling the summer heat intensely because of my imbibing. My old friend Alec had been found guilty of murder several weeks before on July the 1st. A jury of 12 men, hardly Alec's peers, found him guilty of murder in the first degree. An appeal was argued on July 24th for a new trial, based on several court errors made in the jury selection process. The high county court of Carbon overruled that motion. Now it was time for the sentencing phase of judgment. We patiently waited for the judge and his ruling. The drinks from lunch caused me to drift off mentally, back to the time before I first came here to Amerikay. My thoughts took me back to my younger days in Killybegs and Killkenny.

I was born in Killybegs in the year 1820 and as I grew to maturity it soon came time for me to emigrate to another area where I could earn my living and prosper as God intended. The men of my village had been emigrating for years to other lands acquiring wealth and sending money home to keep the folks and the family going. At the age of 18, I left home for the county of Killkenny where I learned the trade of a miner. The next few years for me were very profitable. I sent most of my earnings home to help raise my two younger brothers, Frank and James.

Me Ma died early in the summer of 1844; she had been sick with TB and it eventually took her life. Soon me brothers had grown to manhood and were anxious to join me in the mines at Killkenny. I had hoped they would aspire to higher ambitions, but all they could see was the great money I made. The agreement we all came to was that James would stay home with Da that year and Frank would join me in Killkenny. He would learn the trade of a miner and together we would both see that James would be educated in the good schools. Perhaps he would become a priest, that was always Ma's dream. Besides, James was not suitable for the mines. He was small, very thin, and did not have the upper body strength a miner required. James did possess a high intellect and was destined for something better than coal mining. Upon the end of our conversation James admitted he was relieved he was not going down in the deep dark bowels of the earth.

The next year in school James studied extremely hard and made honors in all his classes. At the colliery in Kilkenny I took Frank under my wing and taught him all the facets of coal mining. He was very good with his hands and had a strong back. In a short time he rose from laborer to miner and then superintendent of the works. As for me, I was happy as a ticket boss for a while. Then they put me to work on the locomotives, hauling coal all over Ireland. While traveling through Ireland, I learned of coal being discovered in Amerikay at a place called Buck Mountain.

One very cold March afternoon in 1845, a strange mist came in off the Irish sea and cursed the land and all of Ireland for the next 7 years to come. Not one potato would grow. An Gorta Mor had swept over Ireland and people were dying from a terrible hunger. The potato crop had failed and other crops were being shipped out of Ireland for foreign shores while the peasants died in the fields and the roads. It was from that hardship that me old Da died in the year 1847. Frank, James, and I buried him in St. Columba's cemetery high on the hill overlooking our village.

In the following months, we pooled our money together, paid the farm off, and sold all the animals for slaughter. In Donegal City I had heard the recruiters from the mines of Buck Mountain were holding a job fair and wanted experienced miners. Frank and I were perfect for that opportunity. James would come along with us, of course. Gaining employment with the Buck Mountain Coal company was an easy task. They were anxious to find well-trained miners for their operations in Pennsylvania. Frank and I were hired on as foremen and James went into training as a telegraph operator.

Life in Buck Mountain was an extremely Spartan existence in those first years. Buck Mountain was a vast lumber camp and coal mining operation. Most of the men lived in huts or tents similar to the military. It wasn't so bad in the fall and summer, but Buck Mountain in the winter is a frozen hell. Our first winter we camped in the tents, an utterly bitter experience. In the second year we were promoted in the works and assigned to the log cabins, sleeping 12 men to a cabin. We worked and slept in shifts around the clock. The bed you slept in was always warm from the man who got out of it an hour before you came home. In our third year at the camp we moved into the hotel at

Buck Mountain. It was a large log structure overlooking the fields where the mules were kept. Inside was a fine the tap room with a central fireplace that took the chill off your bones as the brandy warmed your soul. The rooms were small but comfortable and free from drafts. We slept two to a room. There was hot water and soap 3 days a week for a private bath! Our breakfast was served every morning at 4:30 in the main dining room. Meals were served regularly and Mrs. Raines, the owners wife, packed a lunch everyday consisting of posties and tea. The tea would soon turn cold from the chill of the mines. We soon discovered that on hot summer days the tea was a refreshing treat to our parched lips. Some miners were fortunate enough to find lemons at the company store to flavor the tea. Soon the news of this refreshing summertime drink spread by all the miners to the local villages. We would never enjoy tea hot again as much as we would chilled. James referred to it as "chilled tea."

My brothers and I were gaining some prominence among our fellow miners. Our success in the camp was an example to all the newcomers in Buck Mountain. The men came to us for advice on many matters concerning mining and lumbering. Our company was sought after in the tavern in the evening hours. The owners were considering selling us a breast of coal to work on own our. This meant that we would become mine operators. We still longed for the charms and understanding of an Irish lass. The three of us pined for our younger carefree days in Donegal and the girls we knew at Creeslough.

Once a month, on payday, we would travel down the mountain to Summit Hill and spend the weekend there in a fine hotel owned by Mr. Sweeney. It was there I fell in love with my sweet Katie. She was Mr. Sweeney's sister and unattached. I began courting her on my frequent trips to Summit Hill. On July 4[th,] 1858 we were married at St. Joseph's Church by the Spring Tunnel. Our first year as man and wife were spent at Buck Mountain where my first son Andy was born. By the time Katie gave birth in 1862 to Bridget we were living comfortably in Summit Hill at Spring Tunnel. Many of the Irish were coming into Summit Hill now and gathering in the area around St. Joseph's Church. St. Joe's would give comfort and solace to our families for well over a hundred years to come.

Life was good those first years in Summit Hill, until the Civil War came. We saw many of our sons forcibly dragged off into military service. Some of our lads volunteered for the adventure of becoming a soldier, while others joined up because they hated the mines so much they would rather die in the open than underground. That's when all the troubles began. Groups of Irishmen formed to resist the draft. They were commonly known as "Buckshots." Soldiers were sent into our area to bring stability. We virtually lived under martial law during the war of the states. They would not leave our land for many years to come. I was too old by now for the life of a soldier and I was a valuable member of the mining industry. Morgan Powell would see to it that my name would not be placed on the list of eligible men destined for the draft.

Condy Cannon and James Sweeney were forming a benevolent association in Summit Hill called the Ancient Order of Hibernians, with only the best of our men belonging to it. We banded together in the common cause of friendship, unity, and Christian charity. Our organization would welcome and accommodate all new arrivals from Ireland to town. When a miner was hurt we saw that his wife and children were cared for. If a miner died we saw that he had a proper suit of clothes to be buried in and a fitting wake and burial. Orphan children were often taken in by members families of the lodge and raised as their own. The movement became very popular and membership grew rapidly. There were some in the village who thought we were gaining too much political strength and power. Our association with the Catholic church and secret meetings alarmed the roundheads whom we lived among. They started spreading rumors about our organization. Our lack of temperance didn't help our reputation very much either. The main places of our meetings were in the bush, near the burning mine, or right on the church wall outside the rectory of St. Joseph's. Then James Sweeney offered us the back room at the tavern. Many of our prominent leaders owned taverns throughout the area, which provided our membership with a place to meet regularly. The group was issued a charter by the Commonwealth of Pennsylvania, a lawful and respectable order.

It was common at the time for a man to carry a pistol while traveling in the bush. The area was still wild and dangerous. Mountain lions and black bears roamed the area at will. An occasional lobo wolf or coyote would wander down from the high country. Highwaymen prowled the main roads and often hid out in the bush for protection. There was no formal law and order, only the soldiers and a handful of coal and iron police who weren't much better than the highwaymen. The wild west had nothing on us, except a few Indians; at least they knew who their enemies were by a glance. Consequently, when a man had an argument his pistol was often pulled out to settle the score. Some of our AOH members were involved in circumstances defending themselves and brought up on charges. These events gave our Irish countrymen a bad name in the area and stories were spread that we were up to evil deeds against the Welsh, English and German citizens who originally settled the region.

In 1868, my youngest daughter Annie was born. That was the year Alec and I first met at St. Joseph's Church in Summit Hill. I liked the man from the first day we saw each other. He came to Annie's christening party at Sweeney's Hotel with my wife's cousin, Mara Breslin. Katie and a few of the church women were doing a bit of matchmaking in the matter. Alec and Mara were a perfect couple. She admired him very much for his good looks and strength of character. Alec thought Mara was the prettiest lass in all of Panther Valley and confided in me that he would ask for her hand in marriage one day very soon.

Alec had a plan to be out of the mines and in his own business before he would take a wife and start his family. Over in Tamaqua there was a run-down hotel that Alec would buy at a bargain price and turn it into a profitable business. In the meantime he was living with his cousins, the Campbell's, of that town. He saved every cent he made until he had the down payment and made agreement to purchase the hotel. We all went over before the hotel opened and helped clean up the building. The men of the lodge showed up to patch, repair and rebuild the interior of the hotel. Soon Alec had a fine establishment to be proud of. He not only operated the tavern, but acquired a breast of coal from Harry Whiteknight. Alec hired many of his fellow miners who could not gain work in the Lehigh Coal and Navigation Company's mine operations. With the proceeds from this mine and his bar business he opened another tavern in Storm Hill. Jim Carroll, another miner following in Alec's footsteps, took over the management of

Alec's tavern in Tamaqua. Alec moved to Storm Hill and married Mara. The wedding celebration was a fine affair.

Soon he thought of purchasing a breast of coal in Summit Hill to lease out to unemployed Irish miners. That's when he had harsh words with Superintendent Morgan Powell. Morgan was adamant about not doing business with Alec. There was a vociferous argument one night in Mr. Williamsons store about the matter. Alec had the last word when he dammed Morgan for his obstinance. This public display of Alec's anger would be the ruin of him and his good reputation in and around the Panther Valley.

On a bitter cold December night, Morgan Powell was shot down on the streets of Summit Hill. The act was perpetrated in full view of many citizens. We know for a fact that Alec was in Tamaqua that night attending a meeting of the lodge he belonged to there. Three men were seen rushing over the mountain and out Owl Creek Road towards Tamaqua. No one saw who the murderers were, not even Morgan himself. He thought one of the men looked like "Blue Pat," a miner from Centerville. Patrick was arrested along with another man who also had a loud argument with Morgan at Klotz's stables earlier that day. He was Patrick Gildea. The state could not prove beyond a doubt that either of these men had anything to do with the murder and they were acquitted. Suspicion and doubt were cast on Alec Campbell and his lodge brothers of the Ancient Order of Hibernians (AOH). In the passing years many other men would also be charged with that murder. Patrick O'Donnell did 7 years in prison for his after-the-fact knowledge pertaining to the assassination. Young Johnny Maloy would go on trial for a part he didn't play. The local citizens funded his defense and Johnny was found not guilty. Each time, the prosecution would try to implicate Alec's involvement deeper and deeper. I know for a fact that it was Sam Lewelleyn, because his wife had been having an affair with Morgan. Lewelleyn left the area shortly after the shooting and Mrs. Lewelleyn left town 3 months later when the investigations began.

These were the events that started the rash of shootings and beatings in our region. Groups of Welshmen formed a protective association called the Modocs. Their main purpose was to drive the Irish from Carbon and Schuylkill Counties. The Germans organized into small para-military camps, arming themselves heavily. The Irish coal miners of Kilkenny formed a group called the "Sheet Iron Gang." The AOH of Carbon County did not form any groups of vigilante men. Most of the beatings and shootings were senseless arguments between the ethnic groups. All of the Irish Catholic men were classified as thugs, whatever organization they belonged to. It was Franklin B. Gowen and Benjamin Bannan of Pottsville who dubbed all the Irish Catholic AOH members to be "Molly Maguires." This name would strike fear and hatred wherever it was pronounced. It would soon come to pass, that all the evil doings would be blamed on the Molly Maguires. Gowen would also send groups of his own thugs into the coal region to stir up trouble. The most famous of them was James McParlan or, as we knew him, Jamie McKenna.

When I first found out Jamie was a spy in our midst I couldn't believe it. He ate with my family many a time. We put him up on cold nights when he had no place to go. He almost charmed my Bridgie. She would have no part of him! She said, "Da, be careful of that man, I don't like his manner. There is something not real about him." She emphatically asked that I please warn Alec, too. Jamie asked too many questions about Alec and his business. The day she really flipped out about

Jamie was when he brought that Carrigan fella over from Tamaqua to our house for a drink with me. Bridgie knew Carrigan's reputation very well from the newspapers. He was always being locked up for public drunkenness and beating his wife Fanny. Fanny Higgins was an acquaintance of Katie's and Bridgie overheard how Carrigan would beat her and debase her character in front of the children. Many a time my Katie would try to persuade Fanny to leave Jimmy and join her sister's family in Manchester, Virginia.

Yes, I knew them all. Their paths crossed mine on a daily basis. Little did I know then what was actually going on. We were horrified at the time of Morgan's murder, but not as much as when Officer Yost was gunned down in front of his wife at his home in Tamaqua, 2:00 AM, on the day after the Fourth of July. What has puzzled me all this time is how could they tie Alec into all this mayhem? He was a good man, a good Catholic. Alec was a family man. He had witnessed his children's births and deaths. He could never take a life in cold blood as they had charged him.

The news of McKenna's departure from our land was greeted with great suspicion until one day he showed up in court as a witness for the prosecution. A detective! Bridgie was right! She was always a good judge of character. My head was spinning from the outrageous lies he told in the court room on the witness stand about our fine lads of Erin. What puzzled me more was our lads were not allowed to take the stand in their own defense and answer the accusations levied against their characters. Clearly, from the very beginning, the Molly Maguire trials were fixed. The jury was biased and the defense was hobbled in its efforts to actually defend the miners. The outcome was almost predictable. We would not see justice in this matter at all.

My brother Frank was in town for the trial, waiting to come forward as a witness to Alec's whereabouts during several of the incidents charged against him. After his first day in court waiting to be called, Frank spent the later part of the day at Armbruster's Saloon discussing the case with some of the townsfolk. Frank always got a little too loud and obnoxious after belting down porter and whiskey. He never made it back to his hotel room that night. Two shadowy figures stalked him to the bridge over the Lehigh and took an opportune moment to attack him, tossing Frank into the icy turbulent river below. His body was found the next day at the town landing. I was called to Mauch Chunk to identify his remains. Not a mark was found on him and his purse was full of cash. Two blighters were arrested and detained, but at the inquest they were released and the charges were dropped due to lack of evidence.

We buried Frank in Buck Mountain out on the old Stagecoach Road. His wife and children came to Summit Hill and spent the next few years with me and Katie. Frank's boys all grew to maturity handsomely and were educated in good schools. Young John is a lawyer in Philadelphia; Manus became a priest, and Connor is chief of detectives in New York City. James and Frank were very close in their dealings in the AOH and the union. In fear of his life, James felt he would be next and fled to Canada. We never saw him again.

Frank's wife Kiera was remarried to a German in the town, Hezekiah Haldeman. He was a widower and a good man. He had three sons from his first marriage who needed the gentle touch of a mother. Ironically, Hezekiah's brother, John, would bring demeaning testimony against Alec as to his character and reputation. In the years following John would be shunned by the

Haldeman clan for his hostile participation in the trial of Alec Campbell.

The Judge's gavel fell for the third time as he reconvened the court. I was jarred awake from my long daydream. I had traveled back many years in a few short minutes, remembering what once was. Then the worst news that could reach my ears was read aloud in court. Alec was given the death sentence to be carried out within a few weeks. The courtroom was in an outrage. A small fight broke out in the corridor outside as the coal and iron goons rushed to quell the melee. Katie and Bridgie quickly moved to Mara's side to comfort her along with Alec's sisters Sarah and Annie. Alec was promptly removed from the courtroom. The disturbance in the corridor now moved out onto the street as more and more men gathered in the donnybrook. One small group of young men rushed the guards escorting Alec to the paddy wagon, in an attempt to rescue and free him. They were rocking the wagon with such force as to turn it over on its side.

Just then Captain Peeler of the coal and iron squad fired a volley of shots overhead, then they leveled the weapons at the crowd. Precisely at that instant the Easton Greys marched into the town square with fixed bayonets. From the hill above Captain Linden stood ready with his squad of soldiers. Alec yelled out to the crowd to peacefully go home and not bring any more bloodshed upon the land. Immediately everyone dispersed and went home. Some boarded the train waiting for them at the depot. Others walked up Broadway to their respective hotels and boarding rooms. Finally a small group of Irishmen went into the American Hotel tavern to cool their tempers and quench their thirsts. Peace and quiet behavior prevailed that day and no more riots occurred as the newspapers had predicted.

After an appeal and many delays, Alec was executed in a most brutal manner along with young Ed Kelley, Jack Donohue and Mickey Doyle. That black day was June 21st, 1877, the day that horrified the Irish Catholics in the area. Over in Pottsville, six other Irishmen would offer up their lives to the madness of a modern day witch hunt.

We buried Alec in the following days at St. Joseph's Cemetery near his home in Summit Hill. The wake lasted three days as miners from all over the coal fields came to pay respects to Alec's family. Ten thousand miners and their families climbed the road to Summit Hill in an orderly procession. The train depots were tied up all day with folks arriving from as far away as Pittston, Tremont and Coalcastle. The guesthouses were overrun with boarders who were in town for the funeral. Special black funeral cars were put in service by the Switchback line coming from Mauch Chunk. The LC&C ran trolley after trolley from Tamaqua bringing in the mourners. When the grieving ended we all felt a great loss. The area was wrapped in a deep, silent depression for weeks to come. Mara continued to run the tavern Alec had opened and stayed in the area until her death.

As for me, my heart was broken twice that summer. Two short months after I buried my friend Alec, me dear Annie became very sick and died of the fever. She was only a child in her seventh year of life. We buried her in St. Joe's within view of Alec's final resting place. A few short years later I would bury my beloved Katie beside our Annie after her death from a brain tumor.

In 1893, my son Andrew was killed by a fall of coal at the Spring Tunnel Mine. Only my Bridgie remains with me now, taking good care of her old Da. She married Jim Lamb and he's a good lad. I cherish them both.

Over the years I have lost all my sight from an accident at number six and am left to grope my way through town with a cane. I still look back and remember my friend Alec. Every Sunday I stop by his grave and leave a bouquet of beautiful flowers grown by my daughter Bridgie in her garden. Tis' a handsome marker Mara put up in Alec's honor. The headstone stands over seven feet tall. Gracing the top is a Celtic cross. The inscription is written in Gaelic stating the years of his life and death. I am 77 now and soon they'll be placing me here with Katie and all my friends from Donegal.

Author's notes

Hard times in the 1880's and 90's drove Paddy Brennan to the poor farm. Bridgie was not well enough to take care of him. She began suffering from blackouts that the doctors could not explain. Paddy Brennan died a year later in the poor house at Laurytown. Bridgie and Jim Lamb brought Patrick back to Summit Hill to be buried with Katie, Andrew, and Annie. In a few short years Bridgie passed on from the effects of a brain tumor. Jim Lamb, her husband, died of a broken heart soon after losing Bridgie.

The area is filled with the descendants of Alec and Patrick, who take the time every year to gather with other members of the friends and families of the Molly Maguires. They recall fondly how this group of Irish survived the dreaded potato famine, America's Civil War, and the Molly Maguire era. Some have moved away to areas all over the country. One weekend in June the descendants return and fondly commemorate their Irish ancestors. The gravesites are gone now. The headstones were laid down in the graves and then were covered over with 15 feet of top soil in 1959. Only a chart remains showing the people who were buried there. An aging town historian named Joe "Buck" O'Donnell drew a rough diagram on a 27" by 49" piece of cardboard. When he was finished it he had it framed and presented it to the church as a remembrance of Summit Hills original Irish settlers.

The Hospital That Wouldn't Die

From the Drifton Hospital report No. 21 comes a story about one of the landmarks that played a major role in the life of the Hazleton community over the last 100 years. The hospital served the towns of Harliegh, Jeddo, Drifton, Freeland, Eckley, Highland and Buck Mountain. Its located about three miles from Eckley in the small town of Drifton. In the early days the hospital was known as "Miners Hospital," administering to the burns and cuts of the injured coal miners. The hospital was built and first operated by the Coxe brothers, sons of Tench Coxe who has set the stage for his family's successful venture into coal mining. In 1968 the original construction was still being used as the residence of the Gavinski family. The hospital was made up of two large wards with about 20 beds each. There was also a waiting room, operating room, and a large kitchen. The hospital closed its doors in 1889 when the new Hazleton State Hospital opened for business.

The current owner notes that his present day kitchen was actually the operating room of the old hospital where the walls were painted a dark buff color, rather than white, and the operating table was made of stained wood. The staff consisted of a chief surgeon, a superintendent and a male nurse. There

Figure 16 - The Stone Row. This row of homes was built for the higher level employees of Asa Packer. Railroad engineers were typical of those who lived here.

Figure 17 - A street in Eckley Miners' Village. This was an actual company village provided for miners who had to walk to work.

were no regular nurses, but patients who were well enough assisted other patients in the ward.

Transportation to the hospital was limited; horse drawn wagons carted the injured and the sick from the mines at Eckley, Derringer, Stockton and Tomhicken.

The building has been completely demolished and the land developed for modern day usage. In that guise, a portion of the Drifton Hospital will remain having survived the bygone mining era's human pain, suffering and tragedies — including that of the Molly Maguires.

The Legend of Blue Mountain Devil

When I was a kid and would not go to sleep or was mischievous and misbehaving, my grandpa told me the "Blue Devil" would come and get me in my sleep. This threat would immediately get my attention and cause me to stop whatever I was doing. He would then sit me on his knee and tell me of the "Blue Devil," a creature that lived in Panther Valley when he was a kid.

Long before the American Indians came to Panther Valley another kind of being roamed the valley floor and mountain peaks at will. In his diary Count Von Zinzendorf casually mentions the creature in his travels through what he refers to as St. Anthony's Wilderness. Panther Valley had always been the hunting ground of the Iroquois and Algonquin Indians. They would come to the valley several times a year to hunt bear and mountain lion. Peacefully living in the flat land of Bloomingdale Valley were the tribes of the Mengwe and Mingoes. These groups were made up primarily of hunters and gatherers while a few were farmers. The floor of the Mahoning

Valley was rich and fertile. Their camps were wide and spread out, but well protected. The night sentinels had a field of view that was very extensive. A warning could be given out in plenty of time when strangers appeared. It was only at night they were extremely vulnerable to a surprise attack. Not many native tribes would ever think of attacking another group at night, in fear they would be killed and their soul lost in the dark forever. Or worse yet they might come across the creature they called "Maunkshuk." The beast who walks at night. Even before the Indians lived here the Maunkshuk roamed the land in large numbers. They were thought to be a throwback of civilized man, a species lost in time. Early white settlers called the creature the "Blue Devil" because he roamed the Blue Mountain range and was never seen below the Blue Mountain. Even the early Dutch and German farmers knew of this creature's legend and considered the matter with some thought. Most farmers dwelt in the valleys below the Blue Mountain in Berks and Leigh County. It was considered unsafe to cross the Blue Mountain range and settle in the wilderness. The danger was initially considered to be from the Indians who lived in the woods atop the mountain. If the truth be known, it was fear of the "Blue Devil" who roamed the range from Port Carbon to Mauch Chunk. Not until after the Revolutionary War did the white settler dare to venture over the mountain. In fact many of the patriots were awarded land beyond the mountain in return for payment, an award for serving in the Continental Army. In the firelight of a warm cabin during the dead of winter the legend of the Blue Devil would once again come to life.

The creature was said to stand over seven feet tall. His body was naked and covered with a short mane of black hair. The facial characteristics were very much like those of a man or an African primate. It was a swift moving beast, having been seen in several parts of the area in a single day. The favorite haunt of the devil was in the area of Panther Valley that ranges from the Great Swamp between Tamaqua and Seek to the river in the gorge at Mauch Chunk. It was often spotted crossing the mountain peaks at Sharp Mountain and the Nesquehoning ridge. The devil's primary residence seemed to be that of the area we now call the Broad Mountain. It had also been seen in the mining camps at Eckley, Jeddo and Drifton.

In and around Tamaqua and Summit Hill were many caves the creature would use as temporary shelter while roaming the area. It's not known whether the beast communicated with other like creatures or not. The devil had always been spotted as a lone traveler. No one knew whether it was male or female. One trapper by the name of Abe Haldeman came face to face with the devil at his campfire in West Penn Township. He described its teeth as long and sharp, much like a wild cat. The creature was devouring the blood of a small rabbit as it wandered into the campsite. The fire startled it and it darted off into the deep woods. Abe didn't sleep a wink that night. As soon as dawn came he packed up his gear and fled the area.

The winter of 1776 was one of the coldest and most brutal. It was this year the devil would strike the most. At the outpost of Fort Gnaddehuetten, a sentry was brutally attacked one night, his flesh torn from his throat and the blood drained completely from the corpse. A few short miles away in the gorge at Mauch Chunk a hunter was attacked in the same manner. A hunting party went out the next morning, but only one crazed, battered and beaten Army officer returned two days later. His stories of the devil frightened the settlers in the fort and many made arrangements to leave for Philadelphia in the morning. The officer died later that night. His last words were screams of terror at the horrors he saw his men endure. Their bodies were never found. Travelers in the region would be sure to be back in the fort by nightfall or suffer the consequences.

During this time an Indian encampment was held in the valley and the tribe was attacked by the beast at dawn as the sentry dozed intermittently. The devil took away a young six-year-old child. The tracking party did find the boy's lifeless shell tossed on the rocks at the river. His throat has been torn open and the body was devoid of all its blood. Again two days later in the dead of night the sentry was killed and drained of his blood. Two young children were taken from the camp, their remains were never found, only a gory blood trail and pieces of human flesh were recovered. Within a weeks time the Indian camp was attacked again. Just like before the sentry was taken by surprise and several small children were taken. The tribe was in an outrage, no one wanted to walk the perimeter guard during the night in fear of the beast. From the evidence during the last raid it was determined there must be more that one devil out there. Early the next morning the tribe struck their tents and left the Bloomingdale Valley forever.

It was about this time the German farmers began to cross the Blue Mountain Range and settle in Panther Valley. They decorated their barns and homes with multi-colored hex signs to ward off evil spirits. It was originally believed the Germans were superstitious people and the signs were part of their ignorant fears. Whatever you believe, it is true that never was a German farmer or family attacked on their farm day or night. Many of the original Germans came from places in Europe that were very much like the terrain of Pennsylvania. One other group came from the Carpathian Mountains and they knew very well what kind of monster lived in their valley. Early

Figure 18 - Blue Mountain Devil

curfew laws were passed to keep people safe in their homes at night. Travelers were warned not to be out after dark. Inns would not open their doors to anyone arriving late at night. Coach lines ceased route travel where they were, as the sun began to set. Many churches stayed open night and day as traveler's sanctuaries, temporary shelter from the long dark frightening night. The region lived like this for many years, until the English and Welsh moved in to mine the coal deposits found to be plentiful throughout the valley.

It was the coming of these groups of people that would finally undo the devils reign of terror in Panther Valley. As logging and mining camps filled the area, the devil's range became smaller. There was nowhere it could roam that it wasn't seen and hunted by the villagers. Many tried to track it while other took more drastic measures. Gunter Rother devised a plan to trap it in one of the caves outside the town of Summit Hill. In the cave he placed a live goat to tempt the devil to an easy kill. Once inside, Gunter would close off the cave and set fire to kindling he stacked inside the opening. This was a very dangerous and risky attempt. He could be discovered and ripped to shreds by the creature or accompanying beasts. The villagers still did not know for sure if there was only one devil or more. This plan was almost a full success. The creature entered the cave and devoured the goat, but upon Gunter's approach the beast caught scent of him. Gunter did manage to set fire to the kindling at the mouth of the cave opening, trapping the monster inside. Outside Gunter waited with his rifle in case the beast broke through the burning brush. Inside the cave the creature was incensed and frightened as it scrambled to find another escape route. Deeper in the cave it ran until it fell down a shaft that led to the open pits of the old mine. Once outside, it double backed and crept up on Gunter, attacking him from the rear and slaughtering him brutally. The townsfolk found Gunter laying across the rail tracks of the planes at Number 1. His throat had been slashed and the blood drained from his body.

The fire inside the cave had spread to a vein of hard coal that led down the slope to the quarry at the old mine. This was the start of the great fire in Summit Hill that destroyed much of the lower town and set fire to the open mine pits. The fire would burn almost one hundred years, before burning itself out. Tourists would later come from Mauch Chunk on the Switchback Railroad to see the burning mine. No one ever spoke of the devil that wandered the region.

In my grandfather's day the beast still wandered the region attacking small children, lone travelers and livestock.

Mining in the area became a major industry and would eventually be the cause of the devils demise. On a cold night in December of 1918 the devil crept across the tops of Sharp Mountain looking for prey. It would carefully avoid the burning glow of the old mine at Summit Hill. Shortly before midnight a heavy snow began to fall causing the beast to become disoriented by the monotonous white blanket covering the landscape. The beast wandered aimlessly over the terrain, continually avoiding the heat and glow of the burning mines. It was this event that sent the devil scurrying for cover in a frantic rage. As the creature swiftly moved across the land it had fallen into the funnel of an old coal mine air shaft and fell two hundred feet into the burning pit below.

The villagers had no idea what had happened until the bones of the monster were uncovered some years later. The

Figure 19 - Blue Devil Warning

devil was gone. There were no sightings for at least twenty years. Then in 1948 a woman, while picking coal from a culm bank was attacked and murdered in broad daylight on the slopes of the Nesquehoning Mountains. An eyewitness described the attacker as a large ape-like creature, standing 7-feet tall and running at great speed across the open meadows at Bloomingdale Valley. From Time to time the lone cars of the Switchback would spot the animal from the top of Mount Jefferson outside of Summit Hill.

The last sighting of the devil was in 1975, just outside Jim Thorpe, on a hot summer night. Two fishermen spotted it while coming in off the lake at Mauch Chunk Lake Park. Park Rangers kept an eye out for it and closed the lake all that summer.

The devil hasn't been seen since that summer night. One opinion is the beast has climbed to higher, less-populated elevations of the Appalachian chain, never to be seen again, preying on the abundant wildlife that freely roams the mountainsides of Pennsylvania. Campers and hikers beware, the Devil has been seen on the top of the gorge and in the falls below.

Carrigan's Lament

They call me a squealer, rat and turncoat. Now here I sit in the Mauch Chunk Jail and I would do anything to get out, anything. My life in this country has been no bed of roses. I am illiterate, comical looking and short. Once I was a hero in the Civil War. Does that not count for anything? Many of these dammed Mollies didn't even serve their new country. To think they are calling me a coward! Too many times I have watched men suffer torture and die a horrible death. Some times they were my friends and other times my enemies. I am sick of men and murder. What has it gotten us? Too many good men have died, both in the war and in the coal fields. For what, I ask you all? I can no longer tolerate the madness of the Molly Maguires.

I make no excuses for my behavior, I am responsible for myself alone. Mr. Yost died because of my actions. I could have prevented it, but so could many others involved. Jack Jones was a friend to many of my fellow miners; he helped me find work at the Alaska Colliery in Tamaqua. He helped my brothers find work in the mines too. He didn't deserve to die. Yes, I could have stopped it back then before the insanity started and involved us all. If I talk and tell all that I know, many men will hang from the gallows within the next year. If I remain silent, I will hang with them. The decision is not a difficult one. Jamie has promised me a new life in another place. He has promised to take care of my loved ones if anything happens to me. What do the Mollies offer me? The gang has already turned my wife against me to the point she no longer comes to visit me. It's cold and dark in this dungeon cell. The rats are as big as hounds. I would do anything to get out of here, anything!

From the time my ma died my life has been one violent trip through hell. My old Da was an abusive drunk who beat me frequently, until one day I stood up to him and knocked him on his ass. From that day on I have been on my own, making my way in this land. I was ten years old that year. Neighbors put me up in their barns or, at best, took me in the boarding houses. A boy in the breaker doesn't make much money to live on.

The best thing to ever happen to me was me dear Fanny. The day I met her it was love at first sight. We were a happy family together and yes, sure I'd lose me temper once in a while, but it was the drink that made me do it. Normally, I am a good husband and father. Now I have lost Fanny and the kids. I can't even call my priest to this place. I have been excommunicated by the church, trapped between heaven and hell and no place on earth. I have dammed myself in limbo.

The only people who will have anything to do with me are that bunch from Albright's office. He sends me fresh fruit daily. McParlan brings me tobacco and the newspapers. Asa came by the other day offering me a new suit of clothes for the trial proceedings. Many of my old neighbors and friends in the valley consider me a hero, for speaking out and putting an end to all the mayhem.

I wonder will my children be cursed and suffer for my evil deeds. Will my descendants be cursed to the ends of the earth. I hope one day all this can be forgotten and we can all live in peace again. My cousin in Manchester has offered me a job in his foundry if I ever get out of this mess. I hope to patch up the mess with Fanny and the kids so we can all go to Virginia and start a new life.

I am not afraid of these men who live in the valley. I can stand up to the worst of them, but it's my kids I worry about. I can't always be there to protect them when the other children taunt them with viscous words. My dear Fanny has no one to turn to in her hour of need. The kids are a handful and she needs help with the unruly boys of mine. Her Pa isn't much help, as he is old and gray.

The sheriff is coming again with the barber today and I can get a much needed shave. I worry that the barber isn't some Molly sympathizer and he will try to slit me throat with his straight razor. I have asked for Mr. Kelly from Tamaqua, but the Mollies have threatened him also.

Captain Linden came by today to read the Gazette to me. It seems there is much excitement here in Mauch Chunk. The militia has commandeered the Opera House for their billets. There is much drinking and carousing in the streets after the soldiers are off duty. The whole atmosphere has turned into a circus-like production. The law has this strange belief that in the hills above the prison are a thousand armed Irishmen planning to storm the prison and set us free or shoot us to keep us from talking.

The peeler has just arrived and announced that Mr. Albright, Captain Linden and Mr. Siewers are here to discuss my confession made to Mr. Beard and Shepp, of Tamaqua, upon my capture and to strike a deal with the prosecution. I have been informed that if I don't turn states evidence one of the other men will and it will be me hanging by my neck.

A great deal has been made: for my testimony I will go free with enough money to settle in another state. Fanny and the boys will join me after I get settled. McGowan had found me a job in a blacksmith shop at Manchester Virginia. I can go free as soon as the trials are over. Jamie McKenna came by today and urged to take the deal. He claims Campbell is ready to take the same deal and we will all hang together on that same gallows in the same hour.

A deal has been struck! I will do what I must to survive. I have called the prosecution together for a meeting tomorrow. The peeler will be taking me down to Albright's office for the day. A new suit has arrived for my appearance in court. I haven't seen the light of day for months. Tomorrow I will eat in a restaurant and have a porter or two before they bring me back here at nightfall. McKenna came by today to congratulate me on my decision to co-operate. He brought me fresh fruit and tobacco, the like of which I haven't enjoyed for some time now. Jamie has explained what I am doing to Fanny and he says it's agreed upon by her. She will be by my side through the trial. The local Tamaqua Irish in the South ward are giving her trouble over the matter, and I have asked Mr. Albright to find a place for her and the kids here in Mauch Chunk. He has agreed to look into the matter. In the meantime Mr. Shepp has agreed to put on more vigilantes at the house to protect the family.

God help me for what I am about to do!

Jimmy Carrigan was excommunicated by the Catholic Church for his admitted part in the Molly Maguire conspiracy. In his final days he would take the name of James Hegins and turn to the Methodist Church for solace and comfort. He died a broken man in the late 1890's while working for Mr. Brogan's foundry in Manchester Virginia. His confession and testimony brought about the hanging of 20 men on June 21st 1877, in Carbon and Schuylkill counties. In a strange twist of fate it's the 20 wronged Irishmen whom are remembered today and Jimmy Carrigan is a forgotten man lying in an unmarked grave somewhere in the city of Richmond, Virginia.

The Haldeman Family

In the middle of the 16th century, times and events in Europe were very difficult for the peasants and farmers of the Emme River Valley of Switzerland. People were protesting the state controlled church system and the economics thereof. The hierarchy of the church and government were getting rich and fat from the toil of the farmers, carpenters, millers, stone cutters and general laboring folk who inhabited the region. Many found it impossible to make ends meet and were considering other lands to prosper in.

One dark evening a man heavily cloaked and hooded crept through the darkness of night and nailed his proclamation to the heavy wooden door of the cathedral, which was used as the town bulletin board. The note defied the church and the Pope's infallibility in the matters concerning guidance of Christians in their daily lives. The manifest hanging from a nail brought about great changes in the church. The man was Martin Luther, a Catholic monk who sought to split from the church unless it mended its ways. All over Europe the same feeling towards mother church sprang from Luther's actions. Other religious groups now too splintered away from the mainstream.

Among Luther's rebellious Lutherans were other sects like the Swiss Brethren (Amish), Mennonites, and Dunkards. Each group had much in common, but not enough so they could agree. The new groups were called the Anabaptists meaning second baptizing, or re-baptizing. Many believed that baptism as an infant was meaningless and wrong. They stressed baptismal rites as an adult, joining the church of their own free will. Because of these new beliefs many were executed as heretics and infidels. Strife and mayhem poured all over Europe in the name of religion. Many were put to death for their beliefs, such as Michael Sattler, Felix Manz and Conrad Grebel, all martyrs to the cause of Anabaptist freedom and religion.

The only avenue for the people of the Anabaptist faith was emigration to other, more tolerant lands abroad or in other countries. A great many of them went to Russia, Poland, and parts of Southern Bavaria seeking a better life. Some of the more stout of heart boarded sailing ships in Rotterdam and sailed for the New World to a place they knew as Pensilvania, where William Penn promised religious freedom and harmony for all arrivals.

In 1693 the Mennonites had already established a village just north of Philadelphia, Pennsylvania. They called it by many names, but most commonly the settlement was known as Germantown. It was here in 1727 that Michael Haldeman and his family came from Bern, Switzerland to forge a new life in Germantown. They stayed only a few short years. It appeared that even here in the New World, the Mennonites and Brethren could not agree and get along. Once again Michael and his family moved further West to the Village of St. Peter in Chester County, not at all that far from present day Lancaster County. Here they prospered for many years as farmers and a few of the sons took jobs in the local iron works at Hopewell Village and in the French Creek Mine.

Michael's Haldeman's oldest son, also called Michael, would wander towards the Schuylkill River that passed nearby and watch the rough hewn canal boats drift down the river. The worthy crafts were ladened with coal taken out of the mines in the wilderness region they knew as St. Anthony's Wilderness. Michael would often dream what it must be like as a hand on one of those boats. His brother Jacob Haldeman, however, longed for the industry and excitement of the city life in Philadelphia. He was the son who most often took the farm goods into Philly on market day. Here he would stay a day or so and transact business for the family.

During the years of the Revolution the Swiss Brethren (Amish) at Chester County took no sides or part in the conflict. If a wounded Hessian soldier showed up at their cabin door, they wound take him in and nurse him back to health, while hiding him from the patriots. In turn if a patriot need help and care he too was not turned away. As a result of aiding soldiers of the enemy, many were punished for treason by the prevailing Pennsylvania Government. Some were shot while others were imprisoned, and some were offered an opportunity to serve in the Continental Army. Not too many took this course, as it meant excommunication and shunning from the Amish sect. Most decided to leave the area and seek out life under King George III in Canada. They had all agreed that life under the King's rule was good and in the keeping of their faith, they promised to obey the King in all matters of civil life. Others moved further West to Ohio, Indiana, Illinois and further West to Seattle. Some of the clan eventually found their way to the California Gold Rush of 1849.

The Senior member, Michael Haldeman decided to stay in Chester County and continue his family farm. The youngest son Jacob headed for the Tory green hills of Bucks County and later moved to Philadelphia as a grist mill operator. The oldest son Michael followed his heart's dream and to work on the canal and riverboats transporting coal from the mining camps in the wilderness. Not too many years passed by when Michael decided too look for land on the Blue Mountain and start up a farm. With his wife Sarah he moved to the area of Schuylkill County known as West Penn Township. Here he set up a trading post and traded with the few remaining Mengwe Indians and settlers alike.

To Michael and Sarah was born a son they called Jacob, after Michael's brother whom he never saw again. Many years passed and Jacob grew to manhood. In his 27th year he married Magdalena Meyer, the daughter of a prominent Berks County farmer. They continued the trading post in the wilderness until their death. To this couple was born a son called Abraham Haldeman. After the death of his parents, and in his adult years he sold the trading post and moved closer to the town of Tamaqua. In the town he set up a business as a stone cutter. Later on in his life he ran and operated the Anthracite Hotel in the heart of town at the corner of Pine and Railroad Streets.

Born to Abraham and Magdalena was a son Edward, who was the first of the family to go into coal mining. Edward began his toil in the mines as a "mucker" and finished his mining career as the foreman at the Greenwood breaker. He took a wife, Maria Wertman, of the Lutheran faith and soon left the old ways of the Brethren behind him. The couple gave birth to Frank Haldeman. Frank became a coal miner over his father's objection. Later on in life, he became an engineer for the Reading Railroad.

Frank was the first to marry outside of the Germanic community. He married the daughter of Irish immigrants, Bernard Matthews and Bridgett Martin. The young lasses name was Kate Matthews. To Frank and Kate were born ten children. They were Helen, Mae, John, Harriet, Edward, Anna, Henry, George, Charles and Stella. The children are all gone now, but their kids, now adults in middle age, gather every year for the last twenty-five years, over the Fourth of July holiday weekend, at a picnic to honor and celebrate the memory of Frank Haldeman and all the Haldeman ancestors dating back to Michael Haldeman, born in 1698 in a small farming village outside Bern, Switzerland in the Emme River Valley.

Guns at Lattimer

We were all siting around the bar in Paddy Maley's Saloon the day the miners marched through Coal Patch. Johnny O. and me, Mickey Doyle had just finished a game of darts. We were shooting for drinks. I was pretty sharp that day and shot my best game ever. Over in the corner were two of me best friends, Pat Gallagher and old John Coleman, they were shuffling through a friendly game of dominoes.

From the front porch there came a yell about some men marching on the town. We thought for a moment the soldiers were back to cause more trouble for us. The Army came here during the war of the rebellion and never left. They were first sent to insure Lincoln's Conscription Act would be carried out to the full measure of the law. Often they would march on our town and crack a few skulls. This was the method that Pardee and Markel used to get striking men back into the mines, but we weren't going back this time.

Well over twenty years ago our fathers crawled back to work after the long strike of 1875, only to loose more in pay and conditions. Many of our dads were blacklisted from ever working in the mines again. For many of them it was a choice to leave the region or change occupations. Neither choice came easily.

The worst effects were what happened at the time of the Molly Maguires trials. Irishmen all over the coal fields were being falsely accused of murders they never committed. The shocking end came with the hanging of over 20 miners before it would all calm down, but never go away. Irish families no longer felt safe in their beds at night; as a result there was a great exodus of Irish families from the area.

(For 60 years the story of the Molly Maguires lay under a veil of Irish secrecy. The first exposure to the Molly saga came from George Korson's book on the subject.)

The Union had been busted and unity amongst the miners was temporally shattered. The effort to organize would never end and from time to time the law would claim

Maguireism was flourishing again. The truth was we were getting smarter in dealing with the coal operators. We became artful in dealing with their management personnel at the bargaining table. Slowly we gained concessions, year after year. The newcomers to the region from Italy, Poland and the Slavic countries had joined our fight, giving us the needed strength and solidarity we lacked in the 1870's, when only the Irish led the way. Three of the Irishmen who spearheaded the early struggle were from our part of Schuylkill County. They were Mickey Doyle, Ed Kelly and Jack Donohue. I had been named after Michael Doyle, he was my uncle who was hung at the Carbon County Jail, June 21, 1877. In fact, there were a hundred Michael Doyle's named after him in the years following his execution. We all go by the name Mickey, just to strike fear, bewilderment and confusion into the hearts and minds of the coal operators. They never forgot the Molly Maguires and neither did we. Over the years one labor movement after another formed out of the Mollies ashes. The WBA fell by the wayside, passing on the baton to the Knights of Labor and the feisty Mother Jones'. In another movement miners organized in the Amalgamated Association of Miners of the United States. In due time we would all be called the United Mine Workers. It was this group that would finally bring justice and equity to the miners of the Pennsylvania coal fields. In a show of spirit and unity this poem was written by one of the UMW members:

> Here's to the men of Labor,
>
> That brave and gallant band,
>
> That Corbin and old Swigard
>
> Is trying to disband.
>
> But stick and hang brave union men;

We'll make them rue the day

They thought to break the K of L.

In free Amerikay

Austin Corbin was the president of the Reading railroad in the late 1880's.

The first UMW local was formed in Shamokin in 1892. During the next several years well over 70 more new locals were organized in the coal fields. Johnny Fahy from West Hazleton was the leader of that group. He was most instrumental in gathering the different immigrants together into one unified labor force.

We had been idle these last few weeks in the mines due to an incident at Honeybrook colliery. Gomer Jones the superintendent there, tried to beat a young mule driver by the name of John Bodan with a crow bar. Johnny quickly disarmed the tyrant and put him down on the ground where a group of 30 other mule drivers pounded him, they almost killed the superintendent except for the intervention by soldiers stationed at the breaker. Johnny was arrested for assault and held in jail. As news of this injustice spread throughout the region 800 more miners took to the picket lines. The following day a group of 350 workers marched to every Lehigh and Wilkes-Barre colliery systematically shutting them down.

The strike was spreading rapidly, like a wildfire in an open coal pit. By the end of the week over 3,000 miners had walked off the job in protest of the unjust actions taken by the authorities. Fahy had carefully advised the men not to resort to violence and reminded them of "Black Thursday" so many years ago. The miners of the middle coal lands were tired of the slave driver tactics imposed on them by the founding families of the

Fells, Markles, Pardee's and Coxes. Especially the Coxes, their company was founded by Tench Coxe, one of the founders and framers of the Declaration of Independence. How quickly the founding fathers forgot the rights of others when it came to getting their own wealth and setting up their own personal kingdoms in the wilderness.

The men gathered from all over the eastern middle coal fields and began a march towards Hazleton, where a rally was being held in favor of enhancing the union membership. That's where me an Johnny O. came into the picture. Outside Maley's Saloon we joined the group of miners going from patch to patch, gathering support and growing in size at every coal patch it passed through. It was decided that all the marchers would descend on the village green of a small town called Lattimer. The town had been chosen because the Pardee family had large holdings there. Men were starting out from all parts of the area. The miners from Eckley, Jeddo, and Drifton started out on the road for Lattimer. A group of 1,000 strong organized in MacAdoo and arrived in Hazleton where they were confronted by Sheriff Martin of Luzerne County. He had armed his committee of vigilantes from a shipment of 300 Winchester repeating rifles. The Third Brigade of the Pennsylvania National Guard, commanded by General John Gobin, came in from the northwest side of the city to escort the miners under fixed bayonets.

As we stepped out of Paddy Maley's that September afternoon the cool mountain air swept down through the valley. The long hot days of summer end very quickly in the region once Labor Day passes. While the air is cool and crisp the afternoon sun is equally as warming. It was a good day for the march. From Coal Patch to Hazleton are at least a dozen small patch towns. At each place the residents would come out to greet us and cheer us on. Our entourage grew larger in each town. At Audenreid the owner of the local hotel brought out cold barrels of beer as we gathered for a rest in front of his hotel. Johnny O. and I sat under a Hazlewood tree washing down the coal dust from the back of our throats with the cold Eagle beer. Along the way groups of Irishmen in the march would break out in songs from their county homelands.

The roads were dusty and sometimes rocky. Johnny O. and I kept advancing our position in the march. We wanted to be up front when the line reached Lattimer. Now the sun was directly over head and beating down on our dark wool suits. We removed our jackets and loosened our collars. At this point we began to sweat out the cold beers enjoyed back in Audenreid. Keeping ones hat on was a wise idea, a few who didn't passed out from the effects of the beer and hot autumn sun. The man leading us was a guy we all called Italian Tony. He spoke with a heavy broken accent, occasionally shouting "vendetta." By now we were all feeling a bit woozy and the words spoken in his Italian tongue made a lot of sense to us.

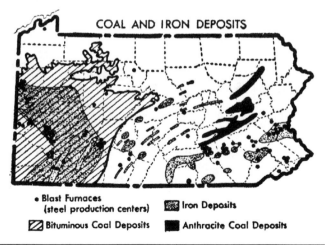

Figure 20 - The immense St. Nicholas Breaker, largest in the world when it was built in 1910.

Figure 21 - Site of the Lattimer Massacre near Hazleton, Pennsylvania. This was a needless and major tragedy for the miners. It occurred on September 10, 1897.

Sheriff Martin tried to stop us in one town, but we marched right through his line of defense. His deputies were comprised of older men from the offices and administration building of Pardee Coal. They weren't used to strenuous labor or being out in the hot sun. Tempers were high among the deputies. After we broke their line the sheriff boarded all his men on the trolleys bound for Lattimer. From our vantage point in the marching line we watched the cars go over the crest of the hill and disappear into the forked streets of the village. News of our coming had reached the residents of the town and all were off the streets. Now I could see the sheriff's men lined up once again, this time blocking the passage of our march. The Third Division of the National Guard stood at the ready with bayonets thrust in our direction. Tony reminded us this was a peaceful march and to abandoned our walking sticks. I had found one that had a beautiful knob on the end much like a shillelagh from old Erin. I hated parting with it so I placed it by a tree so I would remember to pick it up after the rally. Finally our march was halted by armed soldiers on our right and deputized citizens loaded for bear. No one really thought any more would come of it. Johnny O. and I spotted Beers Tavern up ahead and were ready for another brew. By now the dust from the roads had caked on our clothes and crusted in our throats. We knew this day would soon be at an end. What an adventure we were having!

Sheriff Martin stepped forward into the second line of our rank. He picked out an older smaller miner. Holding a gun to the man's head, he demanded we all disperse or he would blow the man's head off. We all knew the old man, he was from over Girardville way. Bill Larkin was his name, he was a pump man at the Ellen Gowen Colliery. The tension in the air was high. All of a sudden the air was quiet, even the birds stopped singing. We could all hear the sheriff speak in gruff terms to the men of the ranks. Sheriff Martin reached with his other hand to take the American flag away from our lead marcher Tony. As Tony resisted and pulled back the body movement caused the hair trigger on Martin's gun to discharge. Larkin had moved out of the way in the nick of time and the bullet only grazed him.

Unfortunately, the round shattered the leg of young Joey Carroll. Tony then jabbed the sharp ornament at the tip of the flag into Sheriff Martin gut. As he fell to the ground his pistol fired once more, dropping two miners standing nearby. All of a sudden all hell broke loose as the deputized citizens fired a volley of steel-cased rounds into the crowd. Men were dropping like flies. I turned to see my friend Johnny O. just as his head exploded in front of me. His limp corpse crumbled to the earth in a pile of torn flesh and gore. He lay on the dusty ground in a pool of dark red blood. I fell to my knees and cried for his loss as I cradled his body in my lap. Mayhem had broken loose in the streets of Lattimer that afternoon. The National Guard did not do all it could to stop the slaughter. Sheriff Martin's men just kept firing into the crowd. I saw Danny Brogan, a 12-year-old breaker boy murdered in front of his father's eyes. The majority of the marching men had scattered all over the town with the deputies in hot pursuit. The lawmen stopped just long enough to draw a bead on their intended targets, like a shooting gallery at the county fair. Soon I was blinded completely by the blood streaming down my head from a gash I received at the end of a soldiers rifle butt. The dust was settling into the pooling blood and caking on the ground where I knelt with Johnny's lifeless body.

The late afternoon air was filled with the smell of gun powder and the sounds of agony. Now the soldiers had joined in the slaughter. I saw with my own eyes several men in blue, skewer the dead with their long razor sharp bayonets. The deputies were singling out men with severe wounds, kicking them in the head and the groin area. Several discharged their weapons into the wounded just to finish them off. I made every effort to drag Johnny O's lifeless body over to a large tree to gain cover and protection from the mob.

As I moved him across the road another soldier singled me out and bashed the small of my back with the butt of his rifle. He turned on me and pointed the sharp blade of his bayonet at my helpless body when a shot rang out. The veteran of many wars fell to the ground, blood streaming out of his mouth and ears. Behind him stood an old Slavic woman with a pistol in her hand that she had take from a deputy who tried to assault her. It was the lady everyone called "Big Mary." She and her band of countrywomen had come to Lattimer when they heard the shots ring out. The deputies were running away now and the soldiers cordoned the area off to make safe the approach for the rescuing wagons.

The towns people of Lattimer were coming out of their homes with hot water and clean bandages. Local men had made makeshift stretchers out of ladders and tent canvas. Help was coming in from all over the area. Neighbors from as far away as Jackson's Patch came to the rescue. A group of volunteer fireman came in from Hazleton. The men at the mines in Eckley and Buck Mountain walked off the job when they heard the news. Many of the wounded were taken to the great hall at the poor farm in Laurytown. All over the coal region the news had spread like wild fire. Miners were walking off the job all over the eastern coal fields in protest of the action. The entire Anthracite community came to the rescue of the dead and wounded miners.

Figure 22 - Woman Mourning

Twenty-five men were killed that day, 49 men were wounded, 24 Poles, 20 Slovaks and 5 Irishmen. The massacre did more to unify the miners of the area than any other single action the operators had perpetrated on the workers. Bodies lay all over the road, shredded by the steel bullets used by the sheriff and his men. The sound of agony and moaning was enough to drive one mad. The sheriff and his gang fled the area and took up in other parts of the country under assumed names. The Third Brigade was reinforced by the Easton Greys; it was thought that more rioting would break out all over the mountain. Calm did come to the area as in the next few days as one funeral after another took place. Thousands came from all over the coal fields to help bury and pay their respects to the dead miners, who were murdered in peaceful protest.

A sham of a trial was held and the sheriff and his men were vindicated of all murders and attacks on the miners; in the name of keeping the peace the bastards were free to walk the streets again. In all their arrogance the sheriff and his deputies went to the Hazle Brewery to celebrate with an afternoon of cheers, toasts and boasts. Hazle Beer soon became known as "Deputies Beer" and the brewery went out of business six months after the trial.

I buried Johnny O. in a little patch town called Mary D. It was the place where he was born. His body lies in the family plot next to the breaker were he first worked.

My wounds healed physically, but emotionally I never recovered. I have taken to strong spirits and will probably die from their effects. During the day I stay sober enough to do a day's work in the Jeddo Mine, but at night after hours, I poison my body and mind with enough porter and whiskey to blot out the memory of the carnage experienced that day I faced the guns of Lattimer.

Author's Notes

On August 23, 1935 Mickey Doyle died and was buried in Saint Joseph's Roman Catholic Cemetery in Summit Hill, Pa., but not before he could relay this story to his youngest son Hugh, who passed it on to me. As of this writing this is the first time the story has been told in detail. Hugh has passed on now too and all that's left are this story and Mickey's shillelagh.

The UMW would again be involved in more strikes in the region, each time gathering new members until their ranks numbered 150,000 members. Finally, they caused the coal companies to see things their way, but no one would ever forget the massacre in Lattimer.

The Night They Drove Titan Down

Dateline Mauch Chunk, Pa: Thursday September 2, 1937

Mauch Chunk Switch-Back Sold at Auction

It was a sad day in Carbon County when the Switch-Back Railroad was sold as scrap iron to the highest bidder. Times were hard for most the general public and concern for the Switch-Back went unnoticed. Even the local newspaper didn't run the story on page one that day. No one missed the Switch-Back until it was too late.

The story begins in 1827 when the original wagon road spilled down from Summit Hill and was constructed out of the wilderness along Lentz's Trail. The cars from the Hill traveled

Figure 23 - Mt. Pisgah Plane

down the gravity road to the coal chutes at Mauch Chunk and were returned by mule power up the same road. All too soon a bottleneck was created by cars returning empty and cars arriving full of coal. An improved roadbed was sorely needed to increase the shipments of coal and keep up with the demand. The plan was to build a return track to the old mines and it was completed in 1845. This idea involved an intricate system of steam engines, incline planes, Barney cars and cross-over rail systems thus called the Switch-Back Railroad.

A two-way track was built to accommodate quicker delivery to the coal markets of New York and Philadelphia. Both planes were double tracked with steam engines housed at the top of each mountain. Mount Jefferson was in Summit Hill sloping down into the Bloomingdale Valley. Over in Mauch Chunk there was Mount Pisgah slopping down the hillside to the chutes at the Lehigh River.

The moving thrust behind the Switch-Back train was the steam powered engines at the top of the two mountains, a steel band system of propelling the Barney cars up the slopes and returning the empty cars back down the slopes. Once over the pinnacle the only motivation was the force of gravity, until the cars reached the Valley of Bloomingdale and once again the Barney cars pushed the train cars up the slope of Mount Jefferson. One of the Barney cars was proudly dubbed "Titan."

Reminiscing back over the hundred years or so of the Switch-Back operation we find the following notes made by riders and observers of the rail system.

Back in 1861 a passenger car service of 12 cars began its operation from Mauch Chunk to Summit Hill. In 1972 the Hauto Tunnel was completed, thus eliminating the need for the cumbersome method of getting coal down off the mountain. Trains and locomotives now transported many more tons of coal to market. It was at this time the company opened up the Switch-Back to passenger service and tourism. The real popularity of the rail system had begun.

People came from all over to ride the natural roller coaster of Carbon County. In 1873, 35,000 people came to Carbon County just to ride the Switch-Back Railroad. Over 100,000 folks came annually during the 1880's.

In 1910 a ride on the Switch-Back costs 50 cents one way. A round trip was 80 cents. By the year 1915 the rolling stock consisted of 10 cars reduced from 15 or more in the 1890's. Ridership was already beginning to fall off. The advent of the automobile made people free to travel at their own will and no longer dependent on the schedule of a rail system. The cars and rails of the Switch-Back were the early victims of the automobile.

Flagstaff Junction was added to the line in 1910 to accommodate the trolley business going up to Flagstaff Park. In 1915 the pool and picnic park area were added enhancing the appeal of the whole Switch- Back system. Enclosed cars were placed on the line in 1912 for comfort in rainy or cooler weather.

As the automobile was responsible for the decline of ridership in the early 1900's, so was it responsible for the renewed enthusiasm in the 1920's. People were encouraged to take auto tours to Mauch Chunk and Glen Onoko to ride the Switch-Back system. For a short time the railroad experienced a new thrust of passengers and final appreciation of the great railroad, now used just for fun and excitement. Too soon came

Figure 24 - Mt. Pisgah Vacation

Figure 25 - The Asa Packer mansion at Jim Thorpe. He made a huge fortune in coal, canals and railroads.

Figure 26 - A contemporary view of downtown Jim Thorpe.

Figure 27 - Henry Packer Mansion. This magnificent house is located adjacent to the Asa Packer Mansion. It was a wedding gift to Harry from his father, Asa Packer.

Figure 28 - View of Jim Thorpe from atop an adjacent mountain.

Figure 29 - A Remnant of the Lehigh Canal at Weissport, Pennsylvania. It is now a park and picnic area.

the stock market crash of 1929 and the last church group excursion on the Switch-Back. Soon the Flagstaff trolley ceased operation and finally closed in 1929. Repairs to the engine houses atop Pisgah and Jefferson amounted to more than the company could afford. Route 209 between Nesquehoning and Mauch Chunk closed in 1931 for a period of 2 years, for road construction and improvements. At 4:30 on October 12, 1933 car number twelve made the final trip from Mauch Chunk to Summit Hill. The era of the Switch-back sounded its last knell.

In the following years scavengers pilfered as much of the iron and steel from the tracks as was possible without being detected.

Then on September 2, 1937 the last of the railway was sold at auction to a Pottsville scrap iron dealer, Isaac Wiener, for $18,000.

Two unsung heroes came forward and tried to save the Switch-Back in its final days. George Richardson had a six-month purchase option, but failed to raise the needed funds in time. Frank Bernhard adopted a resolution in Harrisburg for a rehabilitation project, but was turned down by the Federal government.

This ended the long proud history of the Switch-Back Railroad. In later times the inclined planes would be used for tobogganing and skiing. All that remains now are the right-of-ways and the paths of the old railroad. As you walk along the beautiful tree-lined walkway you can feel the ghosts of the past and hear the roar of the old cars, coming down the mountain, in the imagination of your mind.

Long term tentative plans to resurrect the line have been started and have a goal of one million dollars a mile for the reconstruction of the railroad.

Much of the glory, splendor and beauty are gone now. You can see a model of what the line was like in Jim Thorpe at the Mauch Chunk Museum. Many thanks to Walter Niehoff, whose boyhood dream it was to build this model. Through his fascination with the Switch-Back railroad, the model illustrates the rail system in a diorama of intricate proportions. It's all that is left of the Switch-Back; be sure to catch it the next time you are in Jim Thorpe.

Farewell now to the Switch-Back until sometime in the future when the Switch-Back rises from the ashes and takes us to the burning mine in Summit Hill once again. Until then here are some memories of the Switch-Back Rail Road.

Reviews

"Hard Coal Docket"

For several weeks I had been on the trail of the courthouse records containing the Molly Maguire trials held in Mauch Chunk, in the mid-1870's. It was my understanding that they were still sitting in the basement of the old courthouse in Jim Thorpe. Then came the idea to make a cold phone call to the offices of the courthouse and see what I could find out. Initially I called the wrong number and the young lady there was very cordial and polite. Promptly she transferred me over to the right department. My call found its way to the chambers of Judge John P. Lavelle. His secretary, Roberta Brewster told me she had been involved in transcribing portions of the transcript for the Judge for his new book.

Figure 30 - Judge John Lavelle. He is an author, historian and Senior Judge of the Court of Carbon County.

Roberta turned the call over directly to the Judge, himself. He was very cordial and curious about my interest in the files.

At first I was very nervous, I remembered that a Martin L'Velle was involved with the Molly defense team in Schuylkill County. As we talked I explained my family research project and where it was leading me, namely in the direction of the Molly Maguire saga. Consequently, I told him about my Irish family connection to the region in the period of 1848 to the time of the trials in 1877. It was then we first discussed his new book *Hard Coal Docket*. What a wonderful idea, I thought. He was more than happy to take a few minutes out of his very busy schedule to discuss with me what he knew about the *voire dire* in the Molly trials. We also talked about our Irish heritage and background in the region. The Judge was impressed with what I knew about my own family from that period of time and offered his help in any way.

Our conversation ended and I was very excited about what had just transpired. From that time on my thoughts were of reading his manuscript. Periodically, as I visit Jim Thorpe, I would inquire about the progress of his book with Gwen Gillespie of the Dimmick Library. If you want to know anything about Jim Thorpe just ask Gwen, she is a fountain of valuable information. Several authors have credited her as their main source and inspiration in their research projects.

Early in February I received my advanced copy of *Hard Coal Docket*. My first impressions were "what a great looking book!" The book is a full 8½ by 11 inches in size and about 2 inches thick. I thought it looked very much like an official law book from the Judge's own library.

Gracing the manuscript is Herman Herzog's painting "Mauch Chunk 1872," a beautiful jacket portrait depicting the canal locks, the majestic Lehigh River, and the waterfront scene along Susquehanna Street. The steeple of St. Marks Church can be seen in the shadows of the mountain. Over to the right in the picture you can pick out Asa Packer's humble abode, looming over his fiefdom with the courthouse where he held immense power over the vassals of Carbon County. Far in the background, rising high atop Mt. Pisgah you can see the steam towers of the engine house of the famous Switchback Railroad.

Hard Coal Docket consists of 430 beautifully and masterfully written pages. The illustrations are numerous — there are about 145 different illustrations, ranging from rough, hand-drawn sketches to full-page, full-color lithographic reproductions. The photographs also range from crystal clear monochrome pictures to full color photos. Included are many newspaper clippings from the 1870's about the Molly proceedings and some exhibit charts laying out the jury selection process and just who was selected.

The contents of *Hard Coal Docket* describes the bench and bar in Carbon County from 1843 to the present day. Judge Lavelle begins with William Penn's thoughts on the rights of free men in England and the transplant of his ideas to the new colony he was founding here in the new land. The book describes how Penn laid down ideas for these new concepts to take shape and form in his colony.

It was very interesting to see how the law profession began in this country before the days of college trained lawyers. The Constitution of 1790 required the laymen of the law to serve in a clerkship of a practicing attorney or gentlemen of known abilities for three years. One also had to study the law under a practicing attorney for two years. Another requirement was the service of a clerkship in a neighboring state for another two years. Finally there was a written examination administered by three gentlemen of the law. After all this, it was odd to find lawyers of the time did not make a great deal of money and they had to augment their income with real estate transactions and the sale of insurance policies.

Hard Coal Docket tells how Carbon County came out of parts of Monroe and Northampton Counties. The man chiefly responsible for this was none other that Asa Packer, the major mover and shaker in the region for a very long time.

By the time I reached Chapter 5, I felt a great wealth of knowledge had been absorbed about the early history of the region. In Chapter 5 the text dealt with the era of transition and growth, a period we were all fortunate to experience. Portrayed in this section are several interesting murder cases worth noting. On page 60 an interesting item about a woman being admitted to the bar for the first time in Carbon County. She was Marianne Shutack LaVelle of Nesquehoning. Another interesting item is a section that talks about the 150th anniversary of the court system and the mock trials of the Molly Maguires. This time there occurred a very different outcome in the court proceedings based on the interpretation of today's law and rights of free men and women.

Chapter 6 deals with the three courthouses, their history, demise and reconstruction. On page 82 is a beautiful watercolor painting of the current courthouse circa 1894. If you look very closely you will see the ghostly image of Packer's mansion in the rear of the painting. Although Asa Packer was gone from the scene by 1894, his powerful presence was still felt in the town of Mauch Chunk. Closing out this section is a full page color photograph of the main courtroom, fully restored to the way it looked in 1894.

The next chapter details the history of the old jail, Carbon County's 125-year-old prison. Up to about a year ago it was still in operation as the County lockup. Tom and Betty Lou McBride bought the prison for renovation into a museum. In this chapter we read of the famous handprint of Alec Campbell on the wall. There are modern theories today that the handprint belongs to a Thomas Fisher. However, there are two sources that indicate it is really Alec Campbell's mark. One is the work of George Korson in 1938, called *Minstrels of the Mine Patch* and the other is a book on the Mollies written in 1877, just after the execution of Alec. This text was written by F. P. Dewees in 1877. This is the first telling of the story claiming the mark belonged to Alec Campbell.

One can see Dewees' book today at the Dimmick library. It is kept under lock and key in the vault. The book is a very thin, short account of the proceedings. If you ask Gwen Gillispie she will be more that glad to let you see this text.

In Chapter 8 the Judge gives an excellent account of historical background and biography on each presiding judge from 1843 to current day. Most significant was the "People's Judge," James C. McCready of Summit Hill. He was the son of Thomas McCready and Rebecca Campbell McCready. This gentlemen rose from the ranks of coal miner the highest seat in the county, but never forgot his roots.

Chapter 10 brings us into the mainstream of the 20th century with the computerization of the courthouse, court management and case administration system. To appreciate this new system all one has to do is handle a few of the old court docket books. You can begin to appreciate the importance of Carbon County's entrance into the 21st century. Being a computer enthusiast I was most intrigued by the chapter on the "High Tech Court System" and how it worked.

Chapter 12 explains the inner workings and fee structures of the Bar association. Chapter 13 features the most notable members of the Bar Association over the past 150 years. Of particular note is Milo Dimmick who was responsible for the Dimmick Library in town.

A very special section of the book is written by Kathleen McBride and dedicated to the life and times of Joe Boyle and his newspaper family. Joe and his dad covered the county court system for over 50 years. It was Joe Boyle who encouraged Kathleen to pursue a career in journalism.

Now we come to the jewel in the crown of this manuscript. Chapter 15 is about the Molly Maguire trial, and carefully looks at the jury selection process. This area is masterfully documented and illustrated. Of particular importance is the explanation of Carbon County's social, economic and political climate during this time, which allowed the likes of Asa Packer, Franklin B. Gowen, Charles Albright and Judge Dreher to trample over the rights of free men. The remaining quarter of this book that is dedicated to the Molly trials.

I heartily recommend reading this book for a clearer understanding of the times and the progression of our right to a fair and speedy trial, that we take for granted.

Hard Coal Docket is printed by the Times News of Lehighton and is available at The Treasure Shop at 44 Broadway in Jim Thorpe (telephone number is 717-325-8380). You can also obtain the book from Marianne S. LaVelle Esq.,

Lehighton Professional Building, 401 Mahoning Street, Lehighton, Pa. 18235. The telephone number there is 610-377-0500. It sells for $29.95. (If mailing is required there is an additional $10.00 charge for postage and handling.) This manuscript is a must in everyone's household. I continually use mine as a major reference works in my ongoing research.

Tales of the Mine Country

I have just finished reading an interesting book written by a child of the coal region — *Tales Of The Mine Country* by Eric McKeever. Although Eric is no longer a child, he touched the child of the coal region in my heart. Reading his stories I reminisced and became entranced by his yarns.

The book is a compact 6 by 9 inch manuscript chock full of stories from the Schuylkill County region. It contains 124 easy-to-read pages of interesting material printed in large type. The cover is an eye-catching canary yellow with a pencil sketch of the Old Glenburne Colliery and the worlds largest culm bank in the background. Inside are 29 chapters covering family tales as well as local stories and legends such as the Molly Maguires. To illustrate his musings Eric uses 12 artfully crafted pencil sketches by his son, Edgar McKeever (who also did the illustrations for this book). Besides the sketches he shows 36 great monochrome photographs depicting the life and times of the coal town dwellers. The book makes a handy companion, especially on a rainy day while visiting the sights of Carbon and Schuylkill Counties.

Eric begins with a collection of memories during his childhood circa the 1930's. While the kids growing up in the 30's may have had to face many hardships, I believe they lived in one of the best eras of all time. They had the best of both worlds experiencing the frontier spirit still lingering from the previous century and enduring the passing rites of modern times.

It's this experience that makes this generation appreciative of life and its ups and downs. Their childhood experiences prepared them well for life and now many are sharing their trials and tribulations with us, imparting their wisdom to our hearts and souls. In his tales he conveys feeling for the lives and times of the folks who survived by mining the "black diamonds" that fueled our industrial revolution and powered our defense industry keeping America free.

As the journey starts Eric spins tales of his Uncle George, Pappy and the fireboss. Quickly we learn about the value of mine rats and canaries through amusing stories. Every collection of tales has its sad ones, it is here we learn about the little boy in the Neilsen mine shaft, Pappy's funeral, the Coaltown hearse, unusual uses of dynamite by aging miners, and the little girl from Pittston. Closing out the book is the eerie tale of the handprint on the cell wall at the old jail at Jim Thorpe. The book would make an interesting one-man show in the theater. Every good show ends with a terrific joke and Eric has one called "Daddy Longlegs in the Coffee Grinder," the kids secret joke on adults.

Tales of the Mine Country is available in paperback from Eric McKeever, 8506 Valleyfield Road, Lutherville, MD 21093. It is written and published by Eric and is available for $10.00 (plus $1.00 for postage and handling). He can also be reached on the Internet at Emckeever@aol.com. When you contact him be sure to ask Eric about his newsletter, The Anthracite History Journal.

Growing up in Coal Country

All my life I heard from my aunts and uncles what it was like growing up in the coal region. Too often I thought they were pulling my leg as old-timers often do. Now I find myself believing their stories as I see them in print by authors like Eric McKeever and Louis Poliniak. The latest book I've read is one written by Susan Campbell Bartoletti called *Growing Up in Coal Country*. The book jacket has a striking monochrome photo of a group of breaker boys, standing together as lens of the camera captures their lasting image.

Growing up in Coal Country is an attractive and unique nostalgic look at life in the mine patch illustrated with 86 beautiful black and white photos from the collections of several historical societies and personal family albums. Each picture is descriptively captioned. The work is divided into eight chapters each talking about a different subject of patch life. The final section discusses the legacy of coal country and once again the photo from the jacket appears to remind us what this book is all about: CHILDREN.

Growing up in Coal Country takes us from the boys' first days at the ominous colliery as breaker boys and the dangerous conditions they had to put up with in their daily work. As they grow older in the mine patch they graduate from the breaker to nippers, spraggers and mule drivers. It is an interesting essay about the dangerous working conditions, superstitions and the freedom miners felt in the dark underground caverns.

The dark side of the book discusses the great sadness of the Black Maria and is accompanied by the Avondale mine disaster and the Pittston Twin shaft disaster.

Contained in the final phrases of the book is the last greatest honor of all, the power and solidarity of the STRIKE! Here leaders like Johnny Mitchell, Mother Jones, Clarence Darrow and Teddy Roosevelt come alive in the last great mining struggle.

Described in the closing pages is the legacy of coal country and the lessons learned by those who spent their early childhood, growing up in coal country. Published by Houghton Mifflin Company, Boston 1996. ISBN 0-395-77847-6. $16.95

The last Day of the Northern Field.

Songs by the Donegal Weavers.

Through the lyrics and tunes of old Irish ditties and coal miners ballads comes forward much of the history about the coal region. The group that does this best is the Donegal Weavers, from Wilkes-Barre, Pa. This group maintains a single objective: TO PRESERVE AND PROMOTE THE CELTIC HERITAGE THROUGH MUSIC. This is their 2nd album dedicated to that proposition.

The songs are about the northeastern Pennsylvania coal mining culture, rich in Irish, Scottish and Welsh values.

Here are a few of the great songs on this album. "Sons of Molly Maguire" is a rollicking foot stomping ballad about the injustice Mickey Doyle, Edward Kelly and Alec Campbell were dealt by the coal companies and Carbon County Justice. "Lost Creek" is a tale about a newspaper reporter caught in the midst of a miner's carousing on payday.

The group does an outstanding performance with an instrumental medley called "Old Joe Clark /Liberty /Boil the Cabbage", an American fiddle trilogy.

Another interesting tune on the album is about a gang of river pirates, known as the Schuylkill Rangers, who operated along the canals and rivers of Schuylkill county. The pirates meet up with the tenacious keel boat captain, Peter Berger who brings them down.

There are 19 songs in all on this album that rock and rollick to the Bluegrass beat found rooted in most Irish and Scottish Music.

The members of the Donegal Weavers group are: Ray Stephens, Joseph P. Jones, Emmett Burke, Dr. John Dougherty, Mary Ruth Kelly and George Yeager. For information about this album and their first album called "Work of the Weavers" write: Donegal Weavers, PO box 2820, Wilkes-Barre, PA 18703-2820.

Included with the album is a companion booklet discussing the background of the "Weavers" and origin of their songs. Also included, if you want to sing along, are the lyrics to each song except the instrumentals. To those tunes you can dance around the house.

The group can also be heard live every Friday night, at an informal sitting room in their rehearsal hall in Mountaintop, Pa. If you would like to spend an evening with them call Mr. Joe Jones (717)-824-1703 for arrangements.

Glossary

There are a small number of coal region terms used in this work that may be unfamiliar to those in other parts of the country. A glossary is provided for the reader's convenience.

AOH   The Ancient Order of Hibernians, a social and fraternal order of Catholics similar to other lodges and clubs.

Barney Car   A small wheeled vehicle attached to a steel band used to pull the mine cars, or passenger cars, up the incline of a plane.

Breaker   Specifically, the machine used to crush the large pieces of coal as they were brought out of the mine. Large lumps might weigh several tons. The term "breaker" came to be applied to the building that housed the crushing machine and sorting screens. The first name of these machines and buildings was "cracker", thus "coal crackers" for the natives of coal towns. In West Virginia, the breaker is called a "tipple".

Breast Of Coal   An upward slanting cut made into a vein (layer) of coal so that the loose coal will fall into awaiting mine cars without having to be shoveled from a flat surface into the coal car.

Coal Patch   A village of houses for the miners located within walking distance of the mine. These villages were owned by the mining company, they usually had a company store, church and saloon. The name comes from the garden patches kept by the women to supplement their food from the company store.

Colliery   The collection of buildings, breaker, railroads, fan house, steam house, washery, stable and other necessary outbuildings surrounding the larger mines and including the mine.

Culm Bank   Huge piles of dirt, slate, rock and other waste material left after the coal has been cleaned and graded for size. After a century of mining, some of these piles became the size of the adjacent mountains.

Donnybrook   A free-for-all fight usually occurring at times of much drinking.

Jimmies   The small coal cars used to carry the coal from the mines, also called "dinkies".

Lokie   A small steam engine used to move coal cars at or near the colliery.

Mucker   The worker who shoveled coal into the cars in the mine. This was brutal toil, later it was done by machines.

Peeler   Captain Peeler was an early Coal and Iron Police officer. Mine police came to be called "peelers" in an eponymous manner.

Plane   A steep incline of various lengths. They were used to transport loaded coal cars to a higher elevation, too steep to be negotiated by the steam engines. The loaded cars were pulled up the incline by steam engines. Mt. Pisgah, Ashley and Mahanoy Plane were some famous ones.

Porter An alcoholic beverage something like ale.

Red Tips The raw sore fingertips suffered by the breaker boys from handling rough coal and rocks.

Roundheads A derogatory term directed towards Germans by the Irish for the custom of their wearing hats with round brims. Later the term was applied to any non-Irish.

Shortloading If a coal car was not loaded well above the top of the car, it was called "short-loaded" and was not paid for by the company. This was a judgement call, and was often the source of bitter labor conflict.

Switchback In the steep mountains where anthracite coal was mined, roads and railroad tracks had to ascend or descend the hillside by a series of zig-zag turns. The inclines were far too steep to traverse in a direct route.

WBA The Workingmens Benevolent Association, a very early miners union formed at St. Clair, Pennsylvania in 1868.

JAMES E. HALDEMAN

James Haldeman was born in Tamaqua on July 27, 1943 in coal company housing on Penn Street. His dad and his grandfather were both deep coal miners. In fact, coal mining in his family goes back to the 1820's in West Penn Township. His Irish side of the family came to the United States during the Great Starvation of Ireland and settled in Summit Hill. The men entered the colliery at Number 6. Jim and his family moved away from Tamaqua after the death of his father from black lung in 1948. In 1961 Jim graduated from Bristol High School and attended the RCA Institute where he majored in Electronics. In 1965 he served in the United States Army as a Communications expert attached to the 34th Artillery. He married Joan Connors in 1970 and they have one son, Bryan, who works as a computer consultant. Jim currently works for a major research firm as a computer maintenance technician where he has been employed since 1968. Since 1995 he has been a feature writer for the *Valley Gazette* and in 1996 joined the staff of the *Anthracite History Journal* as the genealogist.

Acknowledgements

I would like to thank everyone who helped me for their assistance. When I began this project, I never intended to write a book. This manuscript is an outgrowth of all the information I gathered while conducting genealogical research in Carbon and Schuylkill Counties.

The following is a list of people I would like to acknowledge for their technical assistance, encouragement and inspiration.

At the top of my list for technical assistance is Gwen Gillespie at the Dimmick Library in Jim Thorpe. Gwen was my very first contact in the region and she gave me my start in learning about the historical background of Carbon County.

Next I would like to thank Fran Navins and her staff at the Carbon County Courthouse archives. A special thanks goes out to Judy Moon and the staff of the Prothonotaries Office in the Courthouse.

At the "Old Jail" Tom McBride sat with me for many an hour discussing the history of the jail and the "Molly Maguires".

Joe McDermott and Father James Ward, both of Summit Hill, were an immense help in discovering my family history at St. Joseph's Church.

Bernie Coleman and Bob Lemasters of Tamaqua were very helpful with background information and details concerning historical events. Bernie has literally been my eyes and ears in Schuylkill County.

Of the people that first encouraged me are Rebecca Veneable of Summit Hill, who always saw a book in what I was doing. Donald Serfass, the author of "Iron Steps", urged me to gather my stories in a single book and have them published.

Genia Miller's theatrical production, "Spirit of the Molly Maguires", inspired me to work on this collection of stories.

My deepest appreciation to Judge John P. LaVelle who was chiefly responsible for introducing me to many people who influenced the direction my work was taking. He is also responsible for the great organization of the Carbon County archives.

Ed Gildea of the *Valley Gazette* gave me the opportunity to showcase my work in his monthly historical publication. He printed my material ranging from a single letter to the editor, that grew into a monthly column called the "Molly Maguire Forum".

Howard Crown of Hatfield, Pennsylvania, was instrumental in making all the Molly stories come to life, with his tour of the area from Jim Thorpe to Locust Gap.

Edgar McKeever is to be congratulated for the outstanding illustrations created for my book.

In Girardville, a warm thank you goes out to Alice Wayne for spending an afternoon telling me about her Grandfather John Kehoe, and showing me all the artifacts from her collection of memorabilia. Her son, Joe Wayne, always made me feel welcome at the Hibernian House when I was in town.

Thanks to Mike Doyle, who is the Mayor of Danville, California, and Dave Sedar of Delaware for getting me started with the first list ever compiled of the members of the Ancient Order of Hibernians (AOH).

A special thanks to all the members of my family for listening to my stories over and over until the point of screaming out loud.

Thanks to my wife Joan for her sage advice and the many hours spent reading, editing and correcting my early drafts.

I would particularly like to thank Patrick Campbell, author of *A Molly Maguire Story*, for reading some of my work and urging me to publish.

I hope you, the reader, will enjoy my fictional journey through time, in a small part of Pennsylvania's Coal, Industrial and Irish History in the coal fields of the 1870's.

Last but not least, a special thank you to Eric McKeever for his faith in me as a writer.

The following group of names are the knowledgeable folks who have contributed in some way or another to my store of information while doing research for this book:

Walter Boyle, John Zuber, Fern Beyer, Bob Dawson, Ben Philips, Bill O'Brien, Tom Symons, Anne Carberry, Rosemary Towle, Anne Hanley, Paul Scherer, Bill Engelhardt, Sarah Roseanne G., Tom Sweeney, Ellen Engelhardt, Ed Crowley, Joe Boyle, Sean Clarke, Buzz McClafferty, John Messina, Tom Ruch, Jill Clayson, Dixie Costenbader, Donna Ahner, John Faust, Joe Mellet, Christine Breslin, Leo Martin, Jean E. Trippett, Nora Campbell, Dale Freudenberger, Jack Shock, John Haldeman, Jim Brennan, Betty Lou McBride, Dan Chinchar, George Harvan, Jack Julo, and Jack Yalch.

EDGAR MCKEEVER, ARTIST

Edgar McKeever is a commercial artist living in the Baltimore area. His remarkable talent was evident as early as elementary school, more so in high school when he began producing salable artworks. In college, at the Maryland Institute of Art, he quickly gained greater recognition. He produced there an award-winning animation film. He is skilled in computer graphics, line drawings, watercolor and oil renderings. He has now turned his attention to writing and illustrating his own science fiction stories. Edgar McKeever may be reached c/o this publisher, he is currently available for illustration assignments by arrangement.